劉毅老師「克漏字測驗講座」上課筆記
2015年4月29日

Test 1

In many Christian countries, people think they should not work on Sundays. They should go to church and rest.

D 1. A. open B. opened
C. close <u>D. closed</u>

☆ on Sundays 在每個禮拜天
= on every Sunday

(比較) on Sunday
① 在禮拜天 (=on this Sunday)
② = on Sundays

I leave for <u>on Sunday</u>.
= on this Sunday

☆ Call me if you have time.
I'm open 24 hours. (我24小時都可以。)
I'm never closed. (我從不打烊。)

People spend time (in) staying at home with their <u>family</u> and friends or going for a walk.

A 2. <u>A. family</u> B. assignment
C. work D. dinner

spend + 時間 + (in) + V-ing

☆ Ladies and gentlemen.
Family and friends. (各位親朋好友。)
What I am today I owe to my parents. (我今天的成就要歸功於我的父母。)
[一口氣背文法 p.156]

中英文化不同，family 包含 relatives，所以不需再說 relatives。

<u>If</u> you visit these countries on Sundays, you will find the towns very quiet.

D 3. A. Although B. Since
C. Before <u>D. If</u>

☆ town ① 鄉鎮 ② 城市 ③ 市區
Taipei is my kind of town.
(台北是我喜歡的城市。)
If you are coming to Taipei, call me when you get in town.
(如果你要來台北，到市區時打電話給我。)

In Germany, stores are not <u>allowed</u> to open on Sundays.

C 4. A. prohibited (禁止) B. confessed (承認)
<u>C. allowed</u> (允許) D. collected (收集)

Only gas stations and shops within the station can be open.

B 5. A. was B. can be
C. is D. has been

☆ only / even / not / just / ⋮ } +N (副詞+名詞) [文寶 p.156]

Of course, there are no 24-hour-a-day and 7-day-a-week convenience stores.

當然，沒有全年無休、24小時營業的便利商店。

☆ 副詞片語+連字號=複合形容詞 (名詞要用單數)

The store is open 24 hours a day.

= It is a 24-hour-a-day store.

People don't go shopping on Sundays.

Test 2

Trees are more important to us than we realize.

Not only are they beautiful, (but) they (also) provide shelter.

shell n 貝殼
shelter n. 避難所；遮蔽處
shade n. 樹蔭 [ʃed]

not only ~ but also 連接二個子句，後面 but also 可省略，或保留其中之一。[文寶 p.467]

They also keep temperatures down on a hot day.

D 6. A. find B. use
C. go D. keep

{ keep temperatures down 控制溫度
keep prices down 控制物價
keep costs down 控制成本 (使其不上升)

They shade us (間接) from the sun (直接) and even clean the air.

C 7. A. in B. with
C. from D. for

shade ~ from 遮住
prevent ~ from 阻止

中 它們替我們遮住陽光，甚至清淨空氣。

Fruit trees give us food, too.

Most trees are very tough

and can last hundreds of

years.

They can withstand cold winters,

hot summers, and even pollution.

C 8. A. promotion 升遷 B. population 人口

C. pollution 污染 D. portion 部分

☆ We are tough. (我們有耐力。)

We are strong. (我們很堅強。)

We can withstand anything.
忍受

Our friendship will last forever

in good times or bad

under any circumstances.

(我們的友誼長存，無論好壞，

在任何情形下。) [澳講式英語 p.3]

One of the most common

trees found in American towns

was the American elm tree.
榆樹

B 9. A. find B. found

C. finding D. are finding

found 源自 (which were) found。

為什麼動詞用 was?

現在美國最常見的樹是 red maple 紅楓樹。
['mepl]

Unfortunately, Dutch elm disease

affected thousands of trees

throughout the United States.

D 10. A. ~~Doubt~~ Doubtfully 懷疑地

B. Undoubtedly 無疑地

C. Fortunately 幸運地

D. Unfortunately 不幸地

affect v. 影響；侵襲

Dutch elm disease 荷蘭榆樹病

Unfortunately 不幸的是

= Sadly

= Regrettably 令人遺憾地

* regretfully 後悔地

Millions of these beautiful trees

had to be cut down.

This left the towns in which
受

they stood empty.
受補

(這使得有這些樹的城鎮，變得

很空曠。)

In some towns all the trees

had to be cut down.

Test 3

Dale Carnegie rose from a
戴爾 卡內基

humble Missouri farm to
簡陋的

international fame because he

found a way to fill a universal
全世界的

human need.

fill / fulfill / meet } a need 滿足需要

It was a need that he first

recognized back in 1906, when
體認

young Dale was a junior at
大三

State Teachers College in

Warrensburg.
沃倫斯堡

D 11. A. admitted B. filled
C. supplied D. recognized
供應 體認

back in 1906 早在1906年
= as early as 1906

freshman 大一
sophomore 大二 (諧音: suffer more)
junior 大三
senior 大四

To get an education, he was
= In order to ~~get an~~,
struggling against many
奮力抵抗
difficulties.

B 12. A. assignment B. education
作業
C. advantage D. instruction
優點 指導

I will work hard.
I will fight.
I will struggle against anything.
奮力抵抗

struggle against 奮力抵抗
= fight against

His family was poor. His father

couldn't afford the room and

board at college, so Dale had to
伙食

ride horseback 12 miles to attend classes.

B 13. A. training B. board
C. teaching D. equipment
裝備

~~room~~ ride horseback 騎馬
= ride on horseback
= ride a horse

board n. 伙食 (= meals)

Studying had to be done

between his farm chores.

A 14. A. between B. during
C. over D. through

choice n. 選擇
chore n. 雜務
choke [tʃok] v. 使窒息

He withdrew from many school
退出

activities because he didn't have

the time or the clothes. He

had only one good suit.

C 15. A. while B. when
C. because D. though

句子分析法，一定要學

每年的大學入學考試，「克漏字」是必考的題型。「學測」考三篇，「指考」考兩篇，再加上「文意選填」，沒有經過練習，很難得高分。**越是害怕的題型，越要加以練習**。習慣考克漏字測驗，也有助於閱讀測驗得高分。

要練習，就要練習新的題目。本書取材自近年來大陸和日本的大學入學試題，這些題目都是命題教授心血的結晶，我們再經過美籍權威教授 Laura E. Stewart 和美籍編輯 Christian Adams 審慎校對。例如，2014 年大陸江蘇卷，有一篇克漏字，出題原文第一句是：Dale Carnegie rose from *the unknown of a Missouri farm* to international fame.... 我們不得不改成：Dale Carnegie rose from ***a humble Missouri farm*** to international fame....，才合乎美國人的習慣。

每一篇文章，我們都一個句子、一個句子分析，劃上修飾線，讓讀者對句子的結構一目了然。**較難的專有名詞，會附上音標**，如 Dale Carnegie〔'del 'kɑrnəgi〕*n.* 戴爾・卡內基，一般人常誤唸成〔'kɑrnədʒi〕。尤其字典上查不到的，我們寫得更清楚。難的單字，會想辦法讓你背下來，如：chore 這個字難背，我們就教你一口氣背：**choice（選擇）– chore（雜務）– choke（使窒息）**。書中前四回，我曾經開過講座，效果極佳，並錄製「克漏字測驗講座實況 DVD」。

如何看書中的修飾線？例如：

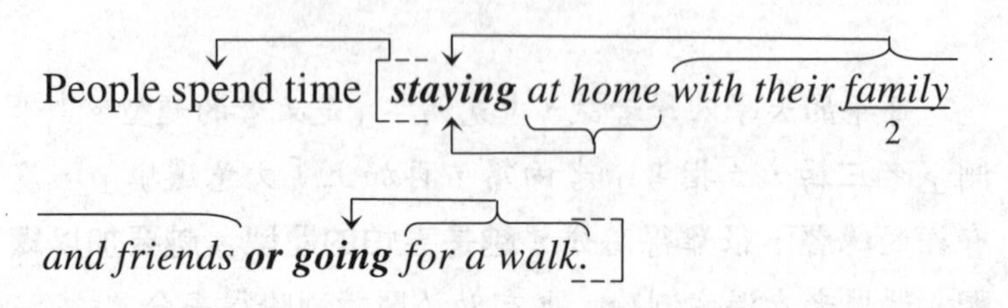

***staying** at home…for a walk* 是省略 in 的「介系詞 + 動名詞」的片語，做副詞片語用，修飾 spend。原則上，修飾語我們用斜細表示，對等連接詞 or 連接兩個動名詞片語，有對稱性，所以用斜黑。at home 是介系詞片語當副詞用，修飾 staying，所以用斜細；with their family and friends 也是介系詞片語，當副詞用，修飾 staying。

這樣一分析就知道，這個句子主幹是 People spend time (in) staying at home or going for a walk. 因此，學會分析句子，可以快速增強英文閱讀能力。**把這本書當成課本一樣，每天唸**，不要看詳解，唸習慣了，你就會考克漏字了。

本書之所能完成，要感謝和我在一起二十多年的蔡琇瑩老師和謝靜芳老師，還有英文才子李冠勳老師的大力協助，全書雖經審慎校對，仍恐有疏漏之處，誠盼各界先進不吝指正。

劉毅

Test 1

Read the following passage and choose the best answer for each blank from the list below.

In many Christian countries, people think they should not work on Sundays. They should go to church and rest. Generally, stores are ___1___ on Sundays. People spend time staying at home with their ___2___ and friends or going for a walk. ___3___ you visit these countries on a Sunday, you will find the towns very quiet. In Germany, stores are not ___4___ to open on Sundays. Only gas stations and shops within the station ___5___ open. Of course, there are no 24-hour-a-day and 7-day-a-week convenience stores. People don't go shopping on Sundays.

【2014 日本大阪經濟大學】

( ) 1. A. open B. opened
C. close D. closed

( ) 2. A. family B. assignment
C. work D. dinner

( ) 3. A. Although B. Since
C. Before D. If

( ) 4. A. prohibited B. confessed
C. allowed D. collected

( ) 5. A. was B. can be
C. is D. has been

Test 1 詳解

(2014 日本大阪經濟大學)

In many Christian countries, people think they should not work *on Sundays*.

在許多基督教的國家裡，人們認爲他們星期天不應該工作。

on Sundays 在每個禮拜天 (= *on every Sunday*)

【比較】 on Sunday ①在禮拜天 (= *on this Sunday*)

②在每個禮拜天 (= *on Sundays*)

They should ***go*** *to church* ***and rest***. 他們應該上教堂和休息。

Generally, stores are closed (1) *on Sundays*.

通常商店在禮拜天不營業 (1)。

1. (**D**) 背三句話，就知道 close 和 open 的用法：

Call me if you have time. (如果你有時間，打電話給我。)
I'm ***open*** 24 hours. (我 24 小時都可以。)
I'm never ***closed***. (我從不打烊。)

open 這個字可當動詞或形容詞，不能用 opened 當形容詞；而 close 當「接近的；親密的」解，作「關閉的」解時，要用 ***closed***，故選 (D)。

People spend time *staying at home with their family and friends or going for a walk.*

人們會和家人和朋友留在家裡，或是出去散步。

「spend + 時間 + (in) + V-ing」，in 通常省略。

2. (**A**) 依句意，選 (A) ***family*** *n.* 家人。而 (B) assignment *n.* 家庭作業，(C) work *n.* 工作，(D) dinner *n.* 晚餐，皆不合句意。

> Ladies and gentlemen.（各位先生，各位女士。）
> Family and friends.（各位親朋好友。）【中外文化不同，不說 relatives（親戚），family 已經包含】
> What I am today I owe to my parents.
> （我今天的成就要歸功於我的父母。）【詳見「一口氣背文法」p.156】

If *you visit these countries on a Sunday*, you will find the towns *very* quiet. 如果你在禮拜天去這些國家，你會發現那些城鎮非常安靜。

3. (**D**) 根據上下文意，選 (D) ***If***「如果」。

town 有時可指「城市」：

town *n.* ①城鎮②城市③市區

【例】Taipei is my kind of ***town***.（台北是我喜歡的城市。）
If you're coming to Taipei, call me when you get in ***town***.（如果你要來台北，到市區時打電話給我。）

In Germany, stores are not allowed to open *on Sundays*.
在德國，禮拜天商店不准營業。

4. (**C**) 依句意，選 (C) ***allowed*** *v.* 允許。而 (A) prohibit *v.* 禁止，除了句意錯以外，prohibited 後面應接 from opening，(B) confess *v.* 承認，(D) collect *v.* 收集，皆不合句意。

Only gas stations ***and*** shops *within the station* can be open.
只有加油站和加油站裡的商店才能營業。

在國外，加油站通常都附有商店。

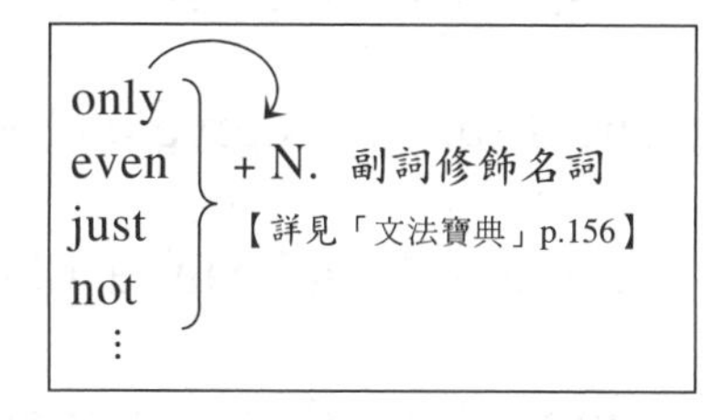

5. (**B**) 依句意，選 (B) ***can be***。

Of course, there are no 24-hour-a-day and 7-day-a-week convenience stores. 當然，沒有全年無休，24 小時營業的便利商店。

副詞片語加連字號，可變成複合形容詞，但要注意，名詞要用單數。例如：

The store is open 24 hours a day.（這家店 24 小時營業。）
= It is a 24-hour-a-day store.

People don't go shopping *on Sundays*. 人們禮拜天不去購物。

Test 2

Read the following passage and choose the best answer for each blank from the list below.

Trees are more important to us than we realize. Not only are they beautiful, but they provide shelter. They also ___1___ temperatures down on a hot day. They shade us ___2___ the sun and even clean the air. Fruit trees give us food, too. Most trees are very tough and can last hundreds of years. They can withstand cold winters, hot summers and even ___3___.

( ) 1. A. find B. use C. go D. keep

( ) 2. A. in B. with C. from D. for

( ) 3. A. promotion B. population C. pollution D. portion

One of the most common trees ___4___ in American towns was the American elm tree. ___5___, Dutch elm disease affected thousands of trees throughout the United States. Millions of these beautiful trees had to be cut down. This left the towns in which they stood empty. In some towns all the trees had to be cut down.

【2014 日本大阪經濟大學】

( ) 4. A. find B. found
C. finding D. are finding

( ) 5. A. Doubtfully
B. Undoubtedly
C. Fortunately
D. Unfortunately

Test 2 詳解
（2014日本大阪經濟大學）

Trees are *more* important to us ***than** we realize.*

樹木對我們的重要性，超出我們所了解的。

Not only are they beautiful, ***but*** they (*also*) provide shelter.
樹木不僅漂亮，而且也提供遮蔽處。

shelter〔'ʃɛltɚ〕*n.* 避難所；掩蔽；遮蔽（= *a place where people are protected from bad weather or from danger*）
背這個字，可先背 shell（貝殼）。
not only…but also 是對等連接詞，連接兩個子句，but 或 also 可以省略，有時兩個都可省略。【詳見「文法寶典」p.467】

They *also* keep temperatures down *on a hot day*.
1
它們在大熱天時，也可以使溫度不要上升。
1

1.（**D**）***keep temperatures down*** 控制溫度（使其不上升）
keep prices down 控制物價（使其不上漲）
keep costs down 控制成本（使其不增加）

They shade us from the sun ***and** even* clean the air. 它們替我們遮住陽光，甚至清淨空氣。
2 / 2

shade〔ʃed〕*n.* 樹蔭 *v.* 遮蔽

一口氣背三個字：
shell *n.* 貝殼
shelter *n.* 避難所
shade *n.* 樹蔭

2.（**C**）shade *v.* 遮蔽 後接 from（使免於），和 prevent…from（阻止…），stop…from（阻止…）用法相同，在間接受詞和直接受詞之間加上 from。

Fruit trees give us food, *too*. 果樹也給我們食物。

Most trees are *very* tough ***and*** can last hundreds of years.
大部份的樹都非常強壯，可以活好幾百年。

tough〔tʌf〕*adj.* 堅強的；強壯的；能吃苦耐勞的

They can withstand cold winters, hot summers ***and*** even pollution.
3
它們可以忍受寒冷的冬天、炎熱的夏天，甚至是污染。
3

withstand *v.* ①抵抗（= *resist*）②忍受（= *endure*）

> We are tough.（我們有耐力。）
> We are strong.（我們很堅強。）
> We can withstand anything.（我們可以忍受任何事。）
>
> Our friendship will last forever in good times or bad under any circumstances.
> （我們的友誼長存，無論甘苦，在任何情況下。）
> 【詳見「演講式英語」p.3】

3.（**C**）依句意，選 (C) ***pollution*** *n.* 污染。
而 (A) promotion *n.* 升遷，(B) population *n.* 人口，
(D) portion *n.* 部份，則不合句意。

One *of the most common trees found in American towns*
4
was the American elm tree.

在美國城鎮裡，最常見的樹木之一，就是美國榆樹。
4

elm〔ɛlm〕*n.* 榆樹

American elm tree

4. (**B**) found 是 *which were* found 的省略。

Unfortunately, Dutch elm disease affected thousands of trees
5
throughout the United States.

不幸的是，荷蘭榆樹病侵襲了全美國數千棵樹。
5

Dutch elm disease 荷蘭榆樹病【小蠹蟲眞菌引起，致葉落枯死】
affect〔ə'fɛkt〕*v.* 影響；侵襲

5. (**D**) 依句意，選 (D) ***Unfortunately*** *adv.* 不幸地。
而 (A) doubtfully *adv.* 懷疑地，
(B) undoubtedly *adv.* 無疑地，
(C) fortunately *adv.* 幸運地，
則不合句意。

Unfortunately = Sadly = Regrettably 令人遺憾地 regretfully 後悔地

Millions of these beautiful trees had to be cut down.
數百萬棵漂亮的樹不得不被砍掉。

This left the towns *in* ***which*** *they stood* empty.
這使得有這些樹的城鎮變得很空曠。

這個句子的主要結構是：This left the towns empty.
主詞 動詞 受詞 受詞補語

stand 的主要意思是「站」，在此作「矗立；屹立；直立生長」解。

In some towns all the trees had to be cut down.
在某些城鎮，所有的樹都必須被砍掉。

Test 3

Read the following passage and choose the best answer for each blank from the list below.

Dale Carnegie rose from a humble Missouri farm to international fame because he found a way to fill a universal human need.

It was a need that he first __1__ back in 1906, when young Dale was a junior at State Teachers College in Warrensburg. To get an __2__, he was struggling against many difficulties. His family was poor. His father couldn't afford the room and __3__ at college, so Dale had to ride horseback 12 miles to attend classes. Studying had to be done __4__ his farm chores. He withdrew from many school activities __5__ he didn't have the time or the __6__. He had only one good suit.

( ) 1. A. admitted B. filled
C. supplied D. recognized

( ) 2. A. assignment B. education
C. advantage D. instruction

( ) 3. A. training B. board
C. teaching D. equipment

( ) 4. A. between B. during
C. over D. through

( ) 5. A. while B. when
C. because D. though

( ) 6. A. permits B. interest
C. talent D. clothes

He tried out __7__ the football team, but the coach turned him down for being too __8__. During this period Dale was slowly __9__ an inferiority complex（自卑感）, which his mother knew could __10__ him from achieving his real potential. She __11__ that Dale join the debate team, believing that __12__ in speaking could give him the confidence and recognition that he needed.

( ) 7. A. on B. for
C. in D. with

( ) 8. A. small B. flexible
C. optimistic D. outgoing

( ) 9. A. finding B. achieving
C. developing D. obtaining

( ) 10. A. prevent B. protect
C. save D. free

( ) 11. A. suggested B. demanded
C. required D. insisted

( ) 12. A. presence B. practice
C. patience D. potential

Dale took his mother's advice, tried desperately, and after several attempts __13__ made it. This proved to be a __14__ point in his life. Speaking before groups did help him gain the __15__ he needed. By the time Dale was a senior, he had won every top honor in __16__. Now other students were coming to him for coaching and they, __17__, were winning contests.

( ) 13. A. hopefully B. certainly
C. finally D. naturally

( ) 14. A. key B. breaking
C. basic D. turning

( ) 15. A. progress B. experience
C. competence D. confidence

( ) 16. A. horse-riding B. football
C. speech D. farming

( ) 17. A. in return B. in brief
C. in turn D. in fact

Out of this early struggle to __18__ his feelings of inferiority, Dale came to understand that the ability to __19__ an idea to an audience builds a person's confidence. And, __20__ it, Dale knew he could do anything he wanted to do—and so could others.

【2014 大陸江蘇卷】

( ) 18. A. convey B. overcome
C. understand D. build

( ) 19. A. express B. stress
C. contribute D. repeat

( ) 20. A. besides B. beyond
C. like D. with

Test 3 詳解

（2014 大陸江蘇卷）

Dale Carnegie rose ***from*** *a humble Missouri farm* ***to*** *international fame* **because** *he found a way to fill a universal human need.*

戴爾・卡內基，從一個簡陋的密蘇里農場，躍升到聞名國際，因爲他找到了一個方法，能滿足全人類的需求。

Dale Carnegie〔'del'kɑrnəgi〕*n.* 戴爾・卡內基【人際關係學大師，Carnegie 這個字常被誤唸成〔'kɑrnədʒi〕】

from A ***to*** B　從 A 到 B　　humble *adj.* 謙虛的；簡陋的；卑微的

fill / ***fulfill*** / ***meet*** / ***satisfy*** } ***a need*** 滿足需要

universal *adj.* 全世界的；普遍的

It was a need [***that*** *he first recognized*[1] *back in 1906*, ***when*** *young Dale was a junior at State Teachers College in Warrensburg.*]

這項需求早在 1906 年，他第一次體認[1]到，當時年輕的戴爾是州立沃倫斯堡師範學院的大三學生。

用 It was…that… 的形式加強 need 的語氣，back in 1906 意思是「早在 1906 年」（= *as early as 1906*）。
freshman「大一新生」，sophomore「大二學生」，junior「大三學生」，senior「大四學生」。
Warrensburg〔ˈwɔrɪnsˌbɝg〕*n.* 沃倫斯堡【在密蘇里州】

1.（**D**）依句意，選(D) ***recognized***。recognize 的主要意思是「認出」，在此解釋爲「體認」。而 (A) admit *v.* 承認，(B) fill *v.* 使充滿，(C) supply *v.* 供應，句意不合。

To get an education, he was struggling against many difficulties.
2

爲了受教育，他奮力抵抗許多困難。
2

To get an education
= In order to get an education
struggle 主要意思是「掙扎」，
struggle against 奮力抵抗
（= *fight against*）

一口氣背：
I will work hard.
I will fight.
I will struggle against anything.

2.（**B**）依句意，選(B) ***education***「教育」。(A) assignment *n.* 家庭作業，(C) advantage *n.* 優點，(D) instruction *n.* 指導，則不合句意。

His family was poor. His father couldn't afford the room and board *at college*, ***so*** *Dale had to ride horseback 12 miles to attend classes*.
3

他的家非常窮。他的父親無法負擔學院的食宿，所以戴爾必須騎 12 哩的馬去上課。
3

ride horseback 騎馬
= ***ride on horseback***
= ***ride a horse***

3. (**B**) board 主要意思是「板子」，「黑板」是 blackboard，由於吃飯要用桌子，所以 board 還指「伙食」（= *meals*）。(A) training *n.* 訓練，(D) equipment *n.* 裝備。

Studying had to be done *between his farm chores.*
4

學習必須在農場的雜務之間完成。
4

chore〔tʃor〕這個字常用複數，指「（家裡或農場的）雜務」，如 household chores「家事」。

一口氣背：
choice *n.* 選擇
chore *n.* 雜務
choke〔tʃok〕*v.* 使窒息

4. (**A**) 依句意，選 (A) ***between***「在～之間」。

He withdrew *from many school activities* ***because*** *he didn't have the time or the clothes*. He had only one good suit.
5 6

他從許多學校的活動中退出，因為他沒有時間或服裝。他只有一套好西裝。
5 6

5. (**C**) 依句意，選 (C) ***because***「因為」。

6. (**D**) 從後句得知，他沒有「服裝」，選 (D) ***clothes***。
(A) permit *n.* 許可證，(B) interest *n.* 興趣，
(C) talent *n.* 天分；才能。

He tried out <u>for</u> (7) the football team, ***but*** the coach turned him down *for being too* <u>*small*</u> (8).

他<u>參加</u>(7)足球隊的甄選，但教練拒絕他，因爲他<u>個子太小</u>(8)。

coach *n.* 教練　***turn down*** 拒絕

7. (**B**) ***try out for*** 參加～的甄選

8. (**A**) 依句意，選 (A) ***small***「個子小的」。
(B) flexible *adj.* 有彈性的；靈活的，(C) optimistic *adj.* 樂觀的，(D) outgoing *adj.* 外向的。

During this period Dale was *slowly* <u>developing</u> (9) an inferiority complex, ***which*** [*his mother knew*] (挿入語) *could* <u>*prevent*</u> (10) *him from achieving his real potential*.

在這段期間，戴爾慢慢地<u>顯現</u>(9)出自卑感，他的母親知道，這樣會<u>阻止</u>(10)他發揮他眞正的潛力。

9. (**C**) 依句意，選 (C) ***developing***。develop 主要意思是「發展」，在此指「顯現」。

10. (**A**) 依句意，選 (A) ***prevent***。

prevent ~ ***from*** 阻止~
= ***stop*** ~ ***from***
= ***keep*** ~ ***from***

prohibit ~ ***from***
= ***discourage*** ~ ***from***
= ***deter*** ~ ***from***

= ***hinder*** ~ ***from***
= ***restrain*** ~ ***from***

complex 主要當形容詞，是「複雜的」，在此當名詞，指「情結」（= *emotional problem*）。

inferiority complex 自卑感；自卑情結
superiority complex 優越感
achieve *one's* ***potential*** 發揮潛力（= *realize one's potential*）

She suggested[11] ***that*** Dale join the debate team, believing ***that*** practice[12] *in speaking* could give him the confidence ***and*** recognition ***that*** *he needed.*

她建議[11]戴爾加入辯論隊，她相信，演說練習[12]能帶給他所需要的自信和認可。

11. (**A**) 依句意，選 (A) ***suggested***「建議」。(B) demand *v.* 要求，(C) require *v.* 要求，(D) insist *v.* 堅持。

12. (**B**) 依句意，選 (B) ***practice***「練習」。

(A) presence *n.* 存在；出席，(C) patience *n.* 耐心。

Dale took his mother's advice, tried *desperately*, ***and after several attempts*** finally made it.
13

戴爾接受他母親的勸告，拼命努力，經過幾次嘗試後，終於成功了。
13

take** sb's **advice 接受某人的勸告 (=*follow sb's advice*)
make it 成功

13. (**C**) 依句意，選 (C) ***finally***「最後」。

(A) hopefully *adv.* 有希望地，(B) certainly *adv.* 必定，(D) naturally *adv.* 自然地。

This proved to be a turning point *in his life*.
14

這證明了是他生命中的轉捩點。
14

14. (**D**) ***turning point*** 轉捩點 (= *critical point*)

Speaking *before groups* did help him gain the confidence *he needed*.
15

在團體面前演說，的確幫助他獲得所需要的信心。
15

15. (**D**) confidence *n.* 自信；信心
(A) progress *n.* 進步 (C) competence *n.* 能力

By the time *Dale was a senior*, he had won every top honor *in speech*. 到了戴爾大四的時候，他已經贏得所有演講的最高榮譽。
16

top honor 最高榮譽（= *top prize*）

16. (**C**) 依句意，選 (C) ***speech*** *n.* 演講。
(A) horse-riding *n.* 騎馬 (B) football *n.* 美式足球
(D) farming *n.* 農耕

Now other students were coming to him *for coaching* ***and*** they, *in turn*, were winning contests.
17

現在，其他學生來找他指導，後來，他們也贏得了比賽。
17

coach 主要作名詞，指「教練」，在此當動詞，指「當教練；指導」。

17. (**C**) ***in turn*** 主要意思是「依序地」，也可指「後來；轉而」。
(A) in return 作爲回報 (B) in brief 簡言之

Out of this early struggle to *overcome* *his feelings of*
18
inferiority, Dale came to understand ***that*** the ability *to* *express*
19
an idea to an audience builds a person's confidence.

從這個早期克服自卑感的努力中，戴爾了解到，能夠向觀眾表達
18 19
想法的能力，可以建立一個人的自信心。

out of 從～中（＝*from*）

18.（**B**）***overcome*** *v.* 克服 (A) convey *v.* 傳達

19.（**A**）***express*** *v.* 表達 (B) stress *v.* 強調
(C) contribute *v.* 貢獻 (D) repeat *v.* 重覆

And, *with* *it*, Dale knew he could do anything *he wanted to do*
20
—***and*** so could others.

而且，有了信心，戴爾就知道，他能夠做到任何他想做的事情——其
20
他人也可以。

20.（**D**）***with*** 有許多意思，在這裡指「具有；附有」（＝*having*）。
【詳見「文法寶典」p.607】
破折號（——）引導總括全句意義的用語，詳見「文法寶典」p.42。

What do we do ***with*** our hands?（手有什麼用？）
What do we do ***with*** English?（英文有什麼用？）

Test 4

Read the following passage and choose the best answer for each blank from the list below.

Joe Simpson and Simon Yates were the first people to climb the west face of the Siula Grande in the Andes mountains. They reached the top __1__, but on their way back conditions were very __2__. Joe fell and broke his leg. They both knew that if Simon __3__ alone, he would probably get back __4__. But Simon decided to risk his __5__ and try to lower Joe down the mountain on a rope（繩）.

( ) 1. A. hurriedly B. carefully C. successfully D. early

( ) 2. A. difficult B. similar C. special D. normal

( ) 3. A. climbed B. worked C. rested D. continued

( ) 4. A. unwillingly B. safely C. slowly D. regretfully

( ) 5. A. fortune B. time C. health D. life

As they ___6___ down, the weather got worse. Then more ___7___ occurred. They couldn't see or hear each other and, ___8___, Simon lowered his friend over the edge of a precipice (峭壁). It was ___9___ for Joe to climb back or for Simon to pull him up. Joe's ___10___ was pulling Simon slowly towards the precipice.

( ) 6. A. lay B. settled C. went D. looked

( ) 7. A. damage B. storm C. change D. trouble

( ) 8. A. by mistake B. by chance C. by choice D. by luck

( ) 9. A. unnecessary B. practical C. important D. impossible

( ) 10. A. height B. weight C. strength D. equipment

___11___, after more than an hour in the dark and the icy cold, Simon had to ___12___. In tears, he cut the rope. Joe ___13___ into a huge crevasse (裂縫) in the ice below. He had no food or water and he was in terrible pain. He couldn't walk, but he ___14___ to get out of the crevasse and started to ___15___ towards their camp, nearly ten kilometers ___16___.

(　) 11. A. Finally　B. Patiently
C. Surely　D. Quickly

(　) 12. A. stand back　B. take a rest
C. make a decision　D. hold on

(　) 13. A. jumped　B. fell　C. escaped　D. backed

(　) 14. A. managed　B. planned　C. waited　D. hoped

(　) 15. A. run　B. skate　C. move　D. march

(　) 16. A. around　B. away　C. above　D. along

Simon had __17__ the camp at the foot of the mountain. He thought that Joe must be __18__, but he didn't want to leave __19__. Three days later, in the middle of the night, he heard Joe's voice. He couldn't __20__ it. Joe was there, a few meters from their tent, still alive.

【2014 大陸全國新課標卷】

(　) 17. A. head for　B. traveled to
C. left for　D. returned to

(　) 18. A. dead　B. hurt
C. weak　D. late

(　) 19. A. secretly　B. tiredly
C. immediately　D. anxiously

(　) 20. A. find　B. believe　C. make　D. accept

Test 4 詳解

（2014 大陸全國新課標卷）

Joe Simpson and Simon Yates were the first people *to climb*.... 喬•辛普森和賽門•葉慈是最初爬上…的人。

Joe〔dʒo〕*n.* 喬　Simpson〔ˈsɪmpsən〕*n.* 辛普森
Simon〔ˈsaɪmən〕*n.* 賽門　Yates〔jets〕*n.* 葉慈

... the west face *of the Siula Grande in the Andes mountains*.
安地斯山脈中大休拉山的西面。

Siula Grande〔sɪˈulə ˈgrænde〕*n.* 大休拉山
Andes〔ˈændiz〕*n.* 安地斯山脈【南美洲】
west face（山的）西面【山的面不用 side，用 face，原題誤用 West Face】

They reached the top successfully (1), ***but*** *on their way back* conditions were *very* difficult (2).
他們成功(1)到達山頂，但是在回程，情況非常艱苦(2)。

1. (**C**) 依句意，選 (C) ***successfully***「成功地」。(A) hurriedly *adv.* 匆忙地。

2. (**A**) 依句意，選 (A) ***difficult***「困難的；艱苦的」。(B) similar *adj.* 相似的，(C) special *adj.* 特別的，(D) normal *adj.* 正常的。

Joe fell ***and*** broke his leg.　喬跌倒，腿摔斷了。

They both knew ***that if*** *Simon* *continued* *alone*, he would *probably* get back *safely*.
3 4

他們兩人都知道，如果賽門單獨繼續走，他可能就會平安回去。
3 4

3. (**D**) 依句意，選 (D) ***continued***「繼續」。因爲是回程往下走，不可選 (A) *climbed*。

4. (**B**) 依句意，選 (B) ***safely***「平安地」。
(A) unwillingly *adv.* 不願意地，(D) regrefully *adv.* 後悔地。

But Simon decided to risk his life ***and*** try to lower Joe *down the mountain on a rope*.
5

但是，賽門決定冒生命危險，努力把喬用繩子垂降下山。
5

and 連接二個不定詞片語 to risk... 和 (to) try to...，做 decided 的受詞。down the mountain（下山）和 on a rope（用繩子）是介詞片語，當副詞用，修飾 lower。

lower *v.* 把～降低

5. (**D**) ***risk*** *one's* ***life*** 冒某人生命危險　(A) fortune *n.* 運氣；財富

As *they* *went* *down*, the weather got worse.
6

當他們下山時，天氣變得更糟。
6

6. (**C**) 依句意，選 (C) ***went***，***go down***「往下走」。(A) lay 的原形是 lie，lie down「躺下」；(B) settle down「坐下；安定下來」，(D) look down「向下看；俯視」。

Then more trouble occurred. 然後，更多麻煩發生。
7 7

7. (**D**) 依句意，選 (D) ***trouble***「麻煩」。原題是 *another trouble*，改成 more trouble 較佳，因爲 trouble 在此爲不可數名詞。

They couldn't see or hear each other ***and***, by mistake, Simon lowered his friend *over the edge of a precipice*.
8
他們彼此看不見也聽不見，結果，一失誤，賽門把他的朋友從峭壁邊緣垂下去。
8

precipice〔ˈprɛsəpɪs〕*n.* 峭壁【諧音：不拉繩必死】

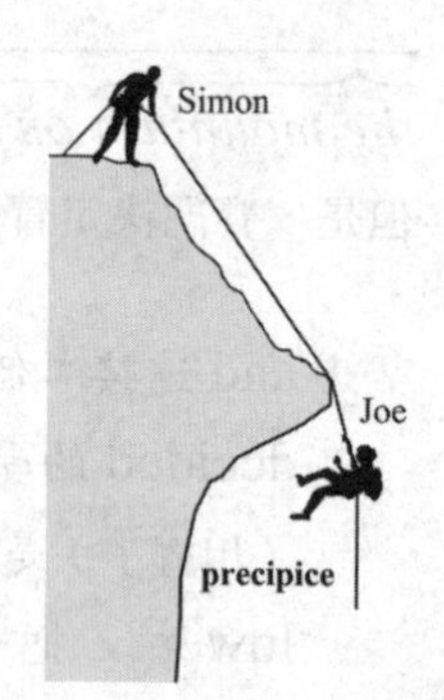

8. (**A**) 依句意，選 (A) ***by mistake***「錯誤地；意外地」(= *by accident*)。而 (B) by chance「偶然地」，(C) by choice「出於自願」，(D) by luck「碰運氣」，則不合句意。

It was impossible for Joe to climb back ***or*** for Simon to pull him up. 喬不可能爬回去，賽門也不可能把他拉上來。
9 9

or 連接二個不定詞片語，做眞正主詞。

9. (**D**) 依句意，選 (D) ***impossible***「不可能的」。

(A) unnecessary *adj.* 不必要的　(B) practical *adj.* 實際的

Joe's weight was pulling Simon *slowly toward the precipice.*
10

喬的重量把賽門慢慢地拉向峭壁。
10

10. (**B**) 依句意，選 (B) ***weight***「重量」。

(A) height *n.* 高度，(C) strength *n.* 力量。

Finally, after more than an hour in the dark and the icy cold,
11
Simon had to make a decision.
12

最後，在黑暗和冰冷中超過一小時之後，賽門必須做出決定。
11　12

in the dark 在黑暗中

in the icy cold 在冰冷中，可以說 ***in the cold***（在寒冷中），但不能說 *in the hot*（誤），要說 ***in the heat***（在炎熱的天氣中）。

11. (**A**) 依句意，選 (A) ***Finally***「最後」。

12. (**C**) ***make a decision*** 做決定

(A) stand back 後退；退縮　(D) hold on 堅持下去

In tears, he cut the rope. 他淚流滿面，把繩子切斷。

in tears 哭泣（= *crying*）

Joe fell into a huge crevasse *in the ice below.*
13

喬掉入下方冰層一個巨大的裂縫裡。
13

crevasse (krə'væs) *n.* 裂縫 (= *a very deep crack in rock or ice*)
【諧音：過肥死，過肥的人擠過裂縫會死】

13.(**B**) 依句意，選(B) ***fell***。　***fall into*** 掉入

He had no food or water ***and*** he was in terrible pain.
他沒有食物和水，而且非常疼痛。【因爲受傷】

He couldn't walk, ***but*** he managed to get *out of the crevasse* ***and***
14

started to move *toward their camp, nearly ten kilometers away.*
15　16

他無法行走，但他設法從裂縫中出來，開始向他們的營地移動，營地在
14　15
將近十公里以外。
16

14.(**A**) ***manage to + V.*** 設法

15.(**C**) 依句意，選(C) ***move***「移動」。
(B) skate *v.* 溜冰，(D) march 行進。

16.(**B**) 依句意，在多遠「以外」，用 ***away***。away 可用於距離和時間，如 ***a week away***「還有一星期」。
The test is still ***a week away***. (離考試還有一星期。)

Simon had returned to the camp *at the foot of the mountain*.
17

賽門回到山腳下的營地。
17

17. (**D**) 依句意，選 (D) ***returned to***。

He thought ***that** Joe must be dead*, **but** he didn't want to leave
18

immediately. 他以為喬一定死了，但他不想立刻離開。
19 18 19

18. (**A**) 依句意，選 (A) ***dead***。

19. (**C**) 依句意，選 (C) ***immediately*** *adv.* 立刻。

Three days later, *in the middle of the night*, he heard Joe's voice. 三天之後，在半夜裡，他聽到喬的聲音。

He couldn't believe it. 他不敢相信。
20 20

20. (**B**) 依句意，選 (B) ***believe***。

Joe was there, *a few meters from their tent*, *still* alive.
喬就在那裡，離他們的帳篷幾公尺，他還活著。

a few meters from their tent 可獨立存在，或是看成副詞片語，still alive 是主詞補語，補充說明主詞 Joe。

Test 5

Read the following passage and choose the best answer for each blank from the list below.

It is often said that breakfast is the most important meal of the day, yet about a quarter of us choose not to eat breakfast. We have food in the kitchen, but we do not feel ___1___ eating first thing in the morning. If we eat our evening meal at six, miss breakfast and have lunch at one, then we have gone nineteen hours between meals. An obvious question is whether long periods between meals use up the brain's energy reserves so that it is unable to perform efficiently. Are we mentally more effective if we eat breakfast than if we miss it?

( ) 1. A. about B. for
C. like D. toward

According to a study, people who did not eat breakfast had poorer memory than people who did. __2__, when people who did not eat breakfast had a drink containing glucose, a type of sugar, their memory was as good as those who had eaten breakfast. If a person eats breakfast, a glucose drink does not further improve memory.

( ) 2. A. Consequently B. However
C. Indeed D. Thus

Based on these and similar findings, it is tempting to suggest that not eating breakfast may result __3__ brain glucose levels falling to the extent that memory is affected. Although the poorer memory of people who have not eaten breakfast is a reason to recommend that a meal be taken first thing in the day, the findings should be kept in context. The improvement in performance is not general and appears to be most strongly associated with memory. The effects are observed when ___4___ demands are placed on the brain's resources. If you are taking a three-hour examination or your job demands that you pay attention to continuous information, then eating breakfast may prove helpful. However, there is only limited evidence that in everyday life a ___5___ to eat breakfast leads to poor performance.

【2014 日本學習院大學】

( ) 3. A. as B. from
C. in D. of

( ) 4. A. considerable B. considerate
C. considered D. considering

( ) 5. A. difficulty B. failure
C. lack D. shortage

Test 5 詳解

（2014 日本學習院大學）

It is often said [***that*** *breakfast is the most important meal of the day*], ***yet*** about a quarter *of us* choose not to eat breakfast.

人們常說，早餐是一天當中最重要的一餐，但是我們當中大約有四分之一的人，選擇不吃早餐。

We have food *in the kitchen*, ***but*** we do not feel like eating *first thing in the morning.*
1

我們在廚房裡有食物，但我們卻不想早上第一件事就是吃東西。
1

first thing in the morning 早上第一件事（= *at the very beginning of the day*）

【例】I will check my e-mail *first thing in the morning.*
（我早上第一件事就是查看我的電子郵件。）

1.（**C**）***feel like*** + ***V-ing*** 想要

[***If*** *we eat our evening meal at six, miss breakfast* ***and*** *have lunch at one*], *then* we have gone nineteen hours between meals.

如果我們六點吃晚餐，沒有吃早餐，一點吃午餐，那麼我們在兩餐之間就連續十九個小時沒吃東西。

go 主要的意思是「去」，在此作「持續」解，如：He ***went*** several days without eating a single thing.（他連續好幾天沒吃一點東西。）

An obvious question is ***whether*** *long periods between meals use up the brain's energy reserves* ***so that*** *it is unable to perform efficiently.*
有個明顯的問題是，兩餐之間相隔很長的時間，是否會用完所儲存的腦力，所以它就無法有效率地運作。

use up 用完　reserve *n.* 儲藏（量）
the brain's energy reserves 所儲存的腦力（= *the brain's supply of energy*）
perform *v.* 執行；表現；工作（= *work*）
efficiently *adv.* 有效率地

Are we *mentally more* effective ***if*** *we eat breakfast* ***than if*** *we miss it*? 是否我們吃早餐比不吃早餐頭腦靈活？

mentally *adv.* 智力上；精神上　effective *adj.* 有效的

According to a study, people ***who*** *did not eat breakfast* had poorer memory ***than*** *people* ***who*** *did.*
根據一項研究顯示，不吃早餐的人比吃早餐的人記憶力差。

However, [***when*** *people* ***who*** *did not eat breakfast had a drink containing glucose, a type of sugar,*] their memory was *as* good ***as*** *those* ***who*** *had eaten breakfast.*

然而，當不吃早餐的人喝了一杯含葡萄糖的飲料，他們的記憶力就和吃過早餐的人一樣好。

glucose〔'glu,kos〕*n.* 葡萄糖

2. (**B**) 依句意，選 (B) ***however*** *adv.* 然而；但是。
而 (A) consequently *adv.* 因此，(C) indeed *adv.* 的確，(D) thus *adv.* 因此，則不合句意。

If *a person eats breakfast*, a glucose drink does not *further* improve memory. 如果一個人吃了早餐，那再喝一杯含葡萄糖的飲料，並不會更加增進記憶力。

Based on these and similar findings, it is tempting to suggest ***that*** *not eating breakfast may result in brain glucose levels falling to the extent* ***that*** *memory is affected.*

根據這些及類似的研究發現，我們會很想指出，不吃早餐，可能會導致大腦葡萄糖含量下降至會影響記憶力的程度。

based on 根據（= *according to*） findings *n. pl.* 研究發現
tempting *adj.* 吸引人的 suggest *v.* 指出
levels *n. pl.* 含量 extent *n.* 程度

3.（**C**）***result in*** 導致 ***result from*** 起因於

Although *the poorer memory of people* ***who*** *have not eaten breakfast* is a reason *to recommend* ***that*** *a meal be taken first thing in the day*, the findings should be kept *in context*.

雖然沒有吃早餐的人記憶力較差，是建議大家每天都吃早餐的理由，但是這些研究結果還是要視情況而定。

context *n.* 上下文；背景；周遭情況；環境
the findings should be kept in context 這些研究結果應視情況而定（= *the information should be considered in relation to the circumstances*）

The improvement *in performance* is not general ***and*** appears to be *most strongly* associated *with memory*.

腦部運作的改善不是全面的，似乎和記憶力最有關連。

be associated with 和～有關

The effects are observed ***when*** <u>*considerable*</u> *demands are placed* 4 *on the brain's resources.*
當非常需要使用腦力的時候，就會注意到這樣的影響。

resources *n. pl.* 資源；儲備力量

4. (**A**) 依句意，選 (A) ***considerable*** *adj.* 相當大的。
而 (B) considerate *adj.* 體貼的，(C) consider *v.* 認為；考慮，(D) considering *prep.* 就…而論；以…看來，則不合句意。

[***If*** *you are taking a three-hour examination* ***or*** *your job demands* ***that*** *you pay attention to continuous information*], *then* eating breakfast may prove helpful. 如果你參加三小時的考試，或是工作時需要注意連續的資訊，那麼吃早餐可能會是很有幫助的。

prove *v.* 證明是

However, there is only limited evidence ***that*** *in everyday life* a <u>failure</u> 5 *to eat breakfast* leads to poor performance.
然而，只有有限的證據顯示，在日常生活中，沒有吃早餐會導致表現變差。

5. (**B**) ***failure to V.*** 未能
(C) lack *n.* 缺乏 (D) shortage *n.* 短缺

Test 6

Read the following passage and choose the best answer for each blank from the list below.

Cultural differences occur wherever you go. When visiting another country, you should be aware of those differences and __1__ them. Here are some __2__ on how to fit in.

( ) 1. A. reject B. recite
C. respect D. remove

( ) 2. A. plans B. tips
C. arguments D. choices

Every traveler to a foreign country feels __3__ at some point. What you do can make locals laugh. Your best defense is a sense of __4__. If you can laugh off eating with the wrong hand in India, locals will warm to you as "that crazy foreigner."

( ) 3. A. unsafe B. excited
C. satisfied D. awkward

( ) 4. A. relief B. belonging
C. humor D. direction

Wearing proper clothes is important too, __5__ locals will judge you by what you wear. In some Middle Eastern countries, exposing your flesh is __6__, especially if you are a woman. So leave your torn jeans at home.

( ) 5. A. but B. for C. so D. or

( ) 6. A. forbidden B. allowed
C. expected D. tolerated

Also be cautious about expressing __7__. Getting angry in Southeast Asia just makes you look silly. In some countries it is __8__ to kiss in public.

【2014 大陸重慶卷】

( ) 7. A. emotions B. concern
C. interest D. views

( ) 8. A. natural B. advisable
C. unwise D. unnecessary

Test 6 詳解

(2014 大陸重慶卷)

Cultural differences occur ***wherever*** *you go*.

無論你去哪裡，都會發生文化差異。

whenever 引導副詞子句，修飾 occur 這個完全不及物動詞。

When *visiting another country*, you should ***be aware of*** those differences ***and*** respect them.
1

當你遊覽另一個國家時，你應該要知道這些差異，並且尊重它們。
1

When *visiting*… 源自 ***When*** *you are visiting*…，副詞子句主詞和 be 動詞句意明確時，可省略。

visit 主要意思是「訪問」，在這裡作「參觀；遊覽」解。

be aware of 知道；察覺到（= *know*）

1. (**C**) re | spect (re = again, spect = look) 從字根分析，respect 意思是「不斷地看」，就是「重視；尊重；尊敬」，依句意選 (C)。

Here are some tips *on **how** to fit in*.
2

這裡有一些關於如何適應環境的祕訣。
2

tip 主要意思是「小費」，在這裡指「祕訣；竅門；訣竅」（= *useful suggestion*）。on 表「關於」（= *about*）。fit 主要意思是「適合」，***fit in*** 字面意思是「可以放進去」，引申爲「適應環境」（= *belong to a situation*）。Here are 是倒裝句，主詞在後面。

2. (**B**) 依句意選 (B) ***tips***。

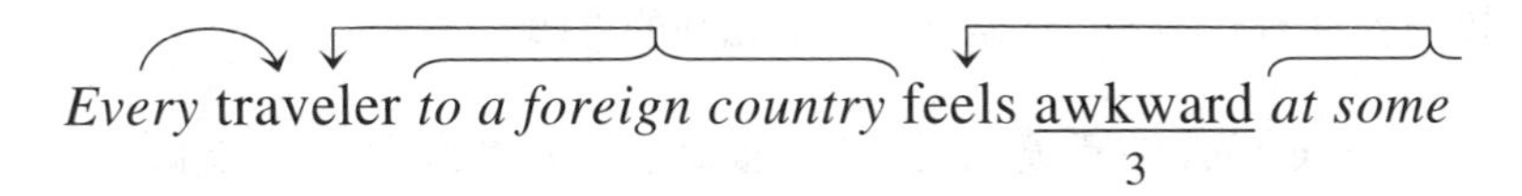

Every traveler *to a foreign country* feels awkward *at some*
3
point. 每個到國外的旅客，都會在某個時候，感到很尷尬。
3

at some point 在某個時候（= *at some time*）

3. (**D**) 依句意選 (D) ***awkward*** *adj.* 不自在的；尷尬的（= *uneasy* = *uncomfortable*）。

***What** you do* can make locals laugh. Your best defense is a
名詞子句
sense *of humor*.
4
你的行爲可能讓當地人笑。你最好的防衛是幽默感。
4

local 主要意思是「當地的；本地的」，在此當名詞，指「當地人；本地人」，如：I'm a local.（我是本地人。）

4. (**C**) 依句意選(C) ***humor*** *n.* 幽默。

a sense of humor 幽默感

***If** you can laugh off eating with the wrong hand in India*, locals will warm to you as "that crazy foreigner".

如果你在印度，吃東西用錯手，自己可以一笑置之而不在意，當地人就會對你有好感，把你當作「那個瘋狂的外國人」。

laugh off 字面意思是「笑著離開」，引申爲「對～一笑置之」（= *laugh away*），含有「不在意」的意思。

warm to 開始喜歡；對～產生好感（= *begin to like*）

Wearing proper clothes is important *too*, ***for** locals will judge you by **what** you wear.*

主詞 (Wearing proper clothes); 5 (for)

穿著適當的衣服也很重要，因爲當地人會根據你的穿著來判斷你。

5 (因爲)

Wearing proper clothes 是動詞片語，做主詞。

for 是對等連接詞，表「原因」，for 表示推斷的理由。

【詳見「文法寶典」p.477 for 和 because 的區別】

5. (**B**) 依句意選(B) ***for***。

In some Middle Eastern countries, exposing your flesh is forbidden, *especially **if** you are a woman*. ***So*** leave your torn jeans *at home*.
6

在某些中東國家，暴露出你的肌膚是被禁止的，尤其是如果你是女人，所以，把你有破洞的牛仔褲留在家裡。
6

so 是轉承語，承接上一句，如果用 Therefore，後面要加逗點。so 很短，所以不加逗點。

6.（**A**）依句意選 (A) ***forbidden***「被禁止的」。
forbid「禁止」的三態為：forbid-forbade-forbidden

Also be cautious *about expressing emotions*. Getting angry *in Southeast Asia just* makes you look silly.
7

也要小心表達出你的情緒。在東南亞，生氣只是讓你看起來很愚蠢。
7

Also 是轉承語，承接上一句。
silly「愚蠢的」（= *foolish* = *stupid*）

7.（**A**）依句意選 (A)，***emotion*** 作「情緒；情感」解，是可數名詞，如：Love, joy, hate, fear and grief are emotions.
（愛、喜、恨、懼和悲都是情緒。）

In some countries it is <u>unwise</u> *to kiss in public*.
8

在某些國家，公開親吻是很<u>不明智的</u>。
8

8. (**C**) 依句意，選 (C) ***unwise***「不明智的」。

un (*not*) + wise (明智的) = unwise (= *foolish*)

it is unwise to kiss in public
= to kiss in public is unwise
it 作爲虛主詞可代替後面的不定詞 to kiss。

【詳見「文法寶典」p.113】

in public「公開地；在衆人面前」(= *publicly*)，有些形容詞可做介詞的受詞，如：

in public (公開地)，in private (私下地)，
in short (簡言之)，in full (詳細地)，
in general (一般而言)，in particular (特別地)，
in vain (徒勞無功)，of late (最近)，
of old (從前)，at large (逍遙法外)，
before long (不久)，for sure (確定地)，
for certain (確定地)，like made (瘋狂地)

【詳見「文法寶典」p.193】

Test 7

Read the following passage and choose the best answer for each blank from the list below.

One night, when I was eight, my mother gently asked me a question I would never forget. "Sweetie, my company wants to ___1___ me but needs me to work in Brazil. This is like your teacher telling you that you've done ___2___ and allowing you to skip a grade（跳級）, but you'll have to ___3___ your friends. Would you say yes to your teacher?" She gave me a hug and asked me to think about it. I was puzzled. The question kept me ___4___ for the rest of the night. I had said "yes" but for the first time, I realized the ___5___ decisions adults had to make.

( ) 1. A. attract　　B. promote
　　　C. surprise　　D. praise

( ) 2. A. little　　B. much
　　　C. well　　D. wrong

( ) 3. A. leave　　B. refuse
　　　C. contact　　D. forgive

( ) 4. A. explaining B. sleeping
C. wondering D. regretting

( ) 5. A. poor B. timely
C. final D. tough

For almost four years, my mother would call us from Brazil every day. Every evening I'd ___6___ wait for the phone to ring and then tell her every detail of my day. A phone call, however, could never replace her ___7___ and it was difficult not to feel lonely at times.

( ) 6. A. eagerly B. politely
C. nervously D. curiously

( ) 7. A. patience B. presence
C. intelligence D. influence

During my fourth-grade Christmas break, we flew to Rio to visit her. Looking at her large ___8___ apartment, I became ___9___ how lonely my mother must have been in Brazil by herself. It was then ___10___ I started to appreciate the tough choices she had to make on ___11___ family and work. She used to tell me that when ___12___ difficult decisions, you wouldn't know whether you made the right choice, but you could always make the best out of the situation, with passion and a ___13___ attitude.

( ) 8. A. comfortable B. expensive
C. empty D. modern

( ) 9. A. interested in B. aware of
C. doubtful about D. satisfied with

( ) 10. A. when B. where
C. which D. that

( ) 11. A. abandoning B. balancing
C. comparing D. mixing

( ) 12. A. depending on B. supplied with
C. faced with D. insisting on

( ) 13. A. different B. friendly
C. positive D. general

Back home, I ___14___ myself that what my mother could do, I could, too. If she ___15___ to live in Rio all by herself, I, too, could learn to be ___16___. I learn how to take care of myself and set high but achievable ___17___.

( ) 14. A. criticized B. informed
C. warned D. reminded

( ) 15. A. managed B. offered
C. attempted D. expected

( ) 16. A. grateful B. energetic
C. independent D. practical

( ) 17. A. examples B. limits
C. rules D. goals

My mother is now back with us. But I will never forget what the ___18___ has really taught me. Sacrifices ___19___ in the end. The separation between us has proved to be a ___20___ for me.【2014 大陆天津卷】

( ) 18. A. question B. experience
C. history D. occasion

( ) 19. A. pay off B. come back
C. run out D. turn up

( ) 20. A. blessing B. gathering
C. failure D. pleasure

Test 7 詳解

（2014 大陸天津卷）

One night, ***when*** *I was eight*, my mother *gently* asked me a question *I would never forget*.

在我八歲時，有一天晚上，我的母親溫柔地問了我一個我永遠都不會忘記的問題。

I would never forget 是省略關代 which 的形容詞子句，修飾 question。

"Sweetie, my company wants to promote (1) me ***but*** needs me to work *in Brazil*.

「親愛的，我的公司想要讓我升遷 (1)，但是需要我去巴西工作。

sweetie〔ˈswitɪ〕*n.* 可愛的人；小可愛
company〔ˈkʌmpənɪ〕*n.* 公司（= *firm* = *corporation* = *enterprise*）
Brazil〔brəˈzɪl〕*n.* 巴西

1.（**B**） pro (forward) | mote (move)　由字根分析，promote 意思是「向前移動」，就是「升遷」，依句意，選 (B)。
而 (A) 吸引，(C) 使驚訝，(D) 稱讚，則不合句意。

This is like your teacher telling you ***that*** *you've done* <u>well</u> ***and***
2
allowing you skip a grade, ***but*** you'll have to <u>leave</u> your
3
friends.

這就像是你的老師告訴你，你表現得<u>很好</u>所以讓你跳級，但是你必須
2
<u>離開</u>你的朋友。
3

and 是對等連接詞，連接文法作用相同的單字、片語或句子。
do〔 du 〕*v.* 表現　　allow〔 ə'laʊ 〕*v.* 允許；讓
skip a grade 跳級

2. (**C**) 依句意，選 (C) ***well*** *adv.* 良好地。

3. (**A**) 依句意，選 (A) ***leave*** *v.* 離開。
而 (B) refuse〔 rɪ'fjuz 〕*v.* 拒絕，
(C) contact〔'kɑntækt 〕*v.* 和…連絡，
(D) forgive〔 fɚ'gɪv 〕*v.* 原諒，則不合句意。

Would you say yes *to your teacher*?" 你會答應你的老師嗎？」

She gave me a hug ***and*** asked me to think about it. I was puzzled.

她給了我一個擁抱，並且要我思考這件事。我很困惑。

say yes to 同意；贊成　　hug〔 hʌg 〕*v.* 擁抱
puzzled〔'pʌzl̩d 〕*adj.* 困惑的（= *bewildered* = *baffled* = *perplexed* = *confused*）

The question kept me <u>wondering</u> *for the rest of the night.*
4

這個問題使我在當晚的其餘時間一直<u>感到疑惑</u>。
4

keep 的基本意思是「保留；保存」，在這裡作「使保持…的狀態；使持續…」解。

rest〔rɛst〕*n.* 剩餘；其餘

4.（**C**）依句意，選 (C) ***wonder***〔ˈwʌndɚ〕*v.* 感到疑惑；憂慮。
而 (A) explain〔ɪkˈsplen〕*v.* 解釋，(B) 睡覺，
(D) regret〔rɪˈgrɛt〕*v.* 後悔，則不合句意。

I had said "yes" ***but*** *for the first time*, I realized the <u>tough</u>
5
decisions *adults had to make.*

我說了「好」，但是我第一次了解到，大人們必須做出<u>困難的</u>決定。
5

for the first time 生平第一次　　realize〔ˈriə,laɪz〕*v.* 了解

make a decision 做決定

5.（**D**）依句意，選 (D) ***tough***〔tʌf〕*adj.* 困難的（= *difficult*）。
而 (A) poor〔pʊr〕*adj.* 差勁的，
(B) timely〔ˈtaɪmlɪ〕*adj.* 適時的，
(C) final〔ˈfaɪnl̩〕*adj.* 最後的，則不合句意。

For almost four years, my mother would call us *from Brazil every day*. *Every evening* I'd eagerly wait for the phone to ring ***and*** *then* tell her every detail *of my day*.
6

近四年來，我的母親每天都會從巴西打電話給我們。每天晚上我都會熱切地等電話響，然後告訴她我一天的每個細節。
6

ring ﹝rɪŋ﹞*v.* (電話)響　detail ﹝ˈditel﹞*n.* 細節

6.(**A**) 依句意，選(A) ***eagerly*** ﹝ˈigəlɪ﹞*adv.* 熱切地。
而(B) politely ﹝pəˈlaɪtlɪ﹞*adv.* 有禮貌地，
(C) nervously ﹝ˈnɝvəslɪ﹞*adv.* 緊張地，
(D) curiously ﹝ˈkjʊrɪəslɪ﹞*adv.* 好奇地，則不合句意。

A phone call, *however*, could *never* replace her presence ***and*** it was difficult *not to feel lonely at times*.
7

然而，一通電話絕不能取代她的存在，而且有時候很難不覺得孤單。
7

phone call 電話　replace ﹝rɪˈples﹞*v.* 取代
lonely ﹝ˈlonlɪ﹞*adj.* 孤單的；寂寞的　***at times*** 有時候

7.(**B**) 依句意，選(B) ***presence*** ﹝ˈprɛzn̩s﹞*n.* 存在。
而(A) patience ﹝ˈpeʃəns﹞*n.* 耐心，

(C) intelligence〔ɪn'tɛlədʒəns〕*n.* 聰明，

(D) influence〔'ɪnflʊəns〕*n.* 影響，則不合句意。

During my fourth-grade Christmas break, we flew to Rio *to visit her.*

在我四年級的聖誕節假期時，我們搭機飛到里約去找她。

grade〔gred〕*n.* 年級　　break〔brek〕*n.* 休假

fly〔flaɪ〕*v.*（搭機）飛行

Rio〔rɪo〕*n.* 里約【巴西城市，全名是 Rio de Janeiro〔'rio də dʒə'nɪro〕*n.* 里約熱內盧】

Looking at her large <u>*empty*</u> *apartment*, I became <u>aware of</u> *how* lonely my mother must have been *in Brazil* by herself.
（8: empty；9: aware of）

看著她偌大<u>空蕩的</u>公寓，我<u>察覺到</u>我的母親自己在巴西必定是多麼的孤單。
（8: 空蕩的；9: 察覺到）

apartment〔ə'partmənt〕*n.* 公寓

8.（**C**）依句意，選 (C) ***empty***「空的」。而 (A) 舒服的，(B) 昂貴的，(D) modern〔'madɚn〕*n.* 現代化的，則不合句意。

9.（**B**）依句意，選 (B) ***aware of***「察覺到…的」。

而 (A) interested〔'ɪntrɪstɪd〕*adj.* 有興趣的 < *in* >，

(C) doubtful〔'daʊtfəl〕*adj.* 懷疑的 < *about* >，

(D) satisfied〔ˈsætɪs,faɪd〕*adj.* 滿意的，則不合句意。

It was *then* ***that*** *I started to appreciate the tough choices she*
10
had to make on *balancing* *family* ***and*** *work.*
11

就在那時候，我開始了解到她必須在使家庭和工作之間取的平衡時，
11
做出困難的選擇。

appreciate〔əˈpriʃɪ,et〕*v.*（正確地）認識；察覺
make a choice 做決定

10.（**D**）此爲「強調句型」，即「It is/was + 強調部份 + that + 其餘部份」，故選 (D)。

11.（**B**）依句意，選 (B) ***balance***〔ˈbæləns〕*v.* 使平衡。
而 (A) abandon〔əˈbændən〕*v.* 拋棄，
(C) compare〔kəmˈpɛr〕*v.* 比較，
(D) mix〔mɪks〕*v.* 混合，則不合句意。

She used to tell me ***that when*** *faced with difficult decisions,*
12
you wouldn't know ***whether*** *you made the right choice*, ***but***
you could *always* make the best out of the situation, *with*
passion ***and*** *a* *positive* *attitude.*
13

她從前告訴我，面對困難的決定，你不會知道你是否做了正確的選擇，
12
但是你總是可以用熱情和正面的態度，在困境中盡力而爲。
13

used to 以前
make the best out of the situation 在困境中盡力而爲
passion〔ˈpæʃən〕*n.* 熱情　　attitude〔ˈætəˌtjud〕*n.* 態度

12.（**C**）依句意，選 (C) ***faced with***「面對」（=*facing*）。
而 (A) depend on「依賴；視…而定」，
(B) supply〔səˈplaɪ〕*v.* 供給 < *with* >，
(D) insist on「堅持」，則不合句意。

13.（**C**）依句意，選 (C) ***positive***〔ˈpɑzətɪv〕*adj.* 正面的。
而 (A) 不同的，(B) 友善的，
(D) general〔ˈdʒɛnərəl〕*adj.* 一般的，則不合句意。

Back home, I reminded myself ***that what*** *my mother could*
14
do, I could, too.
回到家，我提醒自己，我母親能做的，我也可以做到。
14

14.（**D**）依句意，選 (D) ***reminded***「提醒」。
re (*again*) + mind（注意），「再次注意」就是「提醒」。
而 (A) criticize〔ˈkrɪtəˌsaɪz〕*v.* 批評，
(B) inform〔ɪnˈfɔrm〕*v.* 通知，(C) 警告，則不合句意。

If she managed to live in Rio all by herself, I, *too*, could learn to be independent.
15 16

如果她全靠自己設法住在里約，我也可以學會獨立。
15 16

all by *oneself* 獨自；獨助

15. (**A**) 依句意，選 (A) ***managed***「設法」。
而 (B) offer〔ˈɔfɚ〕*v.* 提供，
(C) attempt〔əˈtɛmpt〕*v.* 企圖，
(D) expect *v.* 期待，則不合句意。

16. (**C**) 依句意，選 (C) ***independent***〔ɪndɪˈpɛndənt〕*adj.* 獨立的。
in (*not*) + dependent（依賴的），「不依賴」就是「獨立的」。
而 (A) grateful〔ˈgretfəl〕*adj.* 感激的，
(B) energetic〔ˌɛnɚˈdʒɛtɪk〕*adj.* 充滿活力的，
(D) practical〔ˈpræktɪkl̩〕*adj.* 實際的，則不合句意。

I learn ***how*** *to take care of myself* ***and*** set high ***but*** achievable goals.
17

我學會如何照顧自己，並且設定遠大但是可達成的目標。
17

take care of 照顧　　set〔sɛt〕*v.* 設定
high〔haɪ〕*adj.* 遠大的
achieve（達成）– e + able (*adj.*) = achievable *adj.* 可達成的

17. (**D**) 依句意，選 (D) ***goals***「目標」。

而 (A) 例子，(B) 限制，(C) 規則，則不合句意。

My mother is now back with us. ***But*** I will *never* forget ***what*** *the* <u>*experience*</u> *has really taught me.*
18

我的母親現在回來和我們在一起。但是我絕不會忘記這個<u>經驗</u>眞正教導我了什麼。
18

18. (**B**) 依句意，選 (B) ***experience***「經驗」。而 (A) 問題，(C) 歷史，(D) occasion〔əˈkeʒən〕*n.* 場合，則不合句意。

Sacrifices <u>pay off</u> *in the end.* 犧牲最後都會<u>有</u>所<u>回報</u>。
19 19

sacrifice〔ˈsækrə,faɪs〕*n.* 犧牲

sacr (*sacred*) + ifice (*make*)「犧牲」是一種神聖的行爲。

in the end 最後

19. (**A**) 依句意，選 (A) ***pay off***「有回報」。

而 (B) come back「回來」，

(C) run out「用完」，

(D) turn up「出現」，則不合句意。

The separation *between us* has proved to be a <u>blessing</u> *for me*.
20

我們之間的分離證明對我而言是<u>幸運的事</u>。
20

separate（分開）– e + ion (*n.*) = separation〔,sɛpə'reʃən〕*n.* 分離（= *breakup* = *parting*）

prove〔pruv〕*v.* 證明；證實

prove to be 證明爲～；結果爲～（= *turn out to be*）

to be 可以省略：

【例】This has *proved* (*to be*) *useless*.
（這證明是沒有用的。）

【例】His forecast *turned out to be* quite wrong.
（他的預測最後證明是大錯特錯。）

20.（**A**）依句意，選 (A) ***blessing***〔'blɛsɪŋ〕*n.* 幸福；幸運的事。

常考片語：***a blessing in disguise*** 因禍得福

【例】Disappointments can often turn out to be *blessings in disguise*.
（失望的事常常可能的結果是因禍得福。）

而 (B) gathering〔'gæðərɪŋ〕*n.* 聚會，
(C) failure〔'feljɚ〕*n.* 失敗，
(D) pleasure〔'plɛʒɚ〕*adj.* 樂趣，則不合句意。

Test 8

Read the following passage and choose the best answer for each blank from the list below.

Just days after four people died on Mount Everest during a rush by climbers to take advantage of favorable weather, experts say a similar "traffic jam" scenario could happen again. The four climbers were __1__ approximately 200 who reached the top of the world's highest mountain during the first of only two climbing opportunities — each just two or three days __2__.

( ) 1. A. among B. beside
C. over D. within

( ) 2. A. free B. later
C. long D. together

"Normally the opportunities for reaching the summit might get spread out over a number of days, but what happened this year is the weather was bad" — too little snow, for example, __3__ too much slippery ice exposed — "so teams that might have normally climbed earlier didn't go," said Eric Simonson, Himalaya-program director at a US travel service.

( ) 3. A. covered B. left
C. melted D. was

Having a large number of people attempting to climb together inevitably ___4___ to delays, which on Everest can be deadly. "Whoever's the slowest up at the front will hold up everybody," said veteran climber Ed Viesturs. "By the time some people get to the top, they're tired out, and they've probably climbed for longer than they ___5___, and they've used a lot of the oxygen they depend on for the way down," added Viesturs, who has climbed Everest seven times.【2014 日本學習院大學】

( ) 4. A. answers B. gets
C. happens D. leads

( ) 5. A. could B. planned
C. stayed D. tried

Test 8 詳解

(2014 日本學習院大學)

[*Just days **after** four people died on Mount Everest during a rush by climbers to take advantage of favorable weather,*] experts say a similar "traffic jam" scenario could happen *again.*

有四個人死於攀登埃佛勒斯峰的尖峰時刻期間，此尖峰時刻是由於登山客爲了利用有利的天候所致，山難才過了幾天，專家就說，相同的「塞車」場景可能會再次發生。

Mount Everest (maʊnt ˈɛvərɪst) *n.* 埃佛勒斯峰【世界第一高峰】

The four climbers were among (1) *approximately* 200 [***who** reached the top of the world's highest mountain during the first of only two climbing opportunities — each just two or three days long* (2).]

這四位登山客是在約兩百名的登山客當中 (1)，在第一個攀登機會中，登上世界最高峰，只有兩個攀登機會——每個機會只有兩到三天長 (2)。

deadly *adj.* 致命的（= *fatal* = *mortal* = *lethal*）

1.（**A**）依句意，選 (A) ***among*** *prep.* 當中。

而 (B) beside *prep.* 在…旁邊，(C) over *prep.* 在…上面，(D) within *prep.* 在…當中，則不合句意。

2.（**C**）依句意，選 (C) ***long*** *adv.* 長；久。

"*Normally* the opportunities *for reaching the summit* might get spread out *over a number of days*, ***but what*** *happened this year* is the weather was bad" — *too little snow*, *for example*, *left* (3) *too much slippery ice exposed* —

「一般而言，登峰時機可能要過幾天才會傳播出去，但今年所發生的事，是天氣並不好」——例如，雪太少，使 (3) 太多很滑的冰露出——

a number of days 意思是「一些日子；幾天」。

what 等於 the thing that，what happened this year 的意思是「今年所發生的事」。

3.（**B**）leave 的主要意思是「離開」，在這裡的意思是「使～（處於某種狀態）」。

而 (A) cover *v.* 覆蓋，(C) melt *v.* 融化，(D) was *v.* 是，則不合句意。

"***so*** teams ***that*** *might have normally climbed earlier* didn't go," said Eric Simonson, *Himalaya-program director at a US travel service.*

「因此通常可能會早點來爬山的隊伍並沒有出發，」一家美國的旅行社的喜瑪拉雅專案主任，艾瑞克・西門森說。

program 主要意思是「節目」，在這裡的意思是「計畫；專案」。

Having a large number of people *attempting to climb together inevitably* leads to delays, ***which*** *on Everest can be deadly.*
4

有一大群人企圖一起去登山，將不可避免地導致拖延，這在埃佛勒斯峰可能是會致命的。
4

4. (**D**) 依句意，選 (D) ***lead to***「導致」。而 (A) answer *v.* 回答，(B) get *v.* 得到，(C) happen *v.* 發生，則不合句意。

"***Whoever****'s the slowest up at the front* will hold up everybody," said veteran climber Ed Viesturs.

「在前面任何一個速度最慢的人，會讓所有人都延遲，」資深登山客艾德・威斯德斯說。

up at the front 在前面　　***hold up*** 耽擱；延遲
Viesturs〔vɪ′ɛstɝs〕*n.* 維思特斯

"***By the time*** *some people get to the top*, they're tired out, ***and*** they've *probably* climbed *for longer* ***than*** *they* planned, ***and*** they've used a lot of the oxygen *they depend on for the way down*," added Viesturs, ***who*** *has climbed Everest seven times.*

「到了一些人登上山頂時，他們都累壞了，而且可能爬得比他們所計畫的來得更久，而且也使用了很多他們下山要依賴的氧氣，」爬過埃佛勒斯峰七次的維思特斯補充說。

get to 到達（= *arrive at* = *reach*）
by the time 的意思是「到了…的時候」。
be tired out 累壞了
oxygen〔′ɑksədʒən〕*adj.* 氧氣
depend on 依靠（= *rely on* = *count on*）
add 的基本意思是「增加」，在此作「又說」解。

5.（**B**）依句意，選(B) ***plan***「計畫」。

Test 9

Read the following passage and choose the best answer for each blank from the list below.

Charlotte Whitehead was born in England in 1843, and moved to Montreal, Canada at the age of five with her family. While __1__ her ill elder sister for several years, Charlotte discovered she had a(n) __2__ in medicine. At 18 she married and __3__ a family. Several years later, Charlotte said she wanted to be a __4__. Her husband supported her decision.

( ) 1. A. raising B. teaching C. nursing D. missing

( ) 2. A. habit B. interest C. opinion D. voice

( ) 3. A. invented B. selected C. offered D. started

( ) 4. A. doctor B. musician C. lawyer D. physicist

__5__, Canadian medical schools did not __6__ women students at the time. Therefore, Charlotte went to the United States to study ___7___ at the Women's Medical College in Philadelphia. It took her five years to ___8___ her medical degree.

( ) 5. A. Besides B. Unfortunately
C. Otherwise D. Eventually

( ) 6. A. hire B. entertain
C. trust D. accept

( ) 7. A. history B. physics
C. medicine D. law

( ) 8. A. improve B. save
C. design D. earn

Upon graduation, Charlotte ___9___ to Montreal and set up a private ___10___. Three years later, she moved to Winnipeg, Manitoba, and there she was once again a ___11___ doctor. Many of her patients were from the nearby timber and railway camps. Charlotte ___12___ herself operating on damaged limbs and setting ___13___ bones, in addition to delivering all the babies in the area.

( ) 9. A. returned B. escaped
C. spread D. wandered

( ) 10. A. school B. museum
C. clinic D. lab

( ) 11. A. busy B. wealthy C. greedy D. lucky

( ) 12. A. helped B. found
C. troubled D. imagined

( ) 13. A. harmful B. tired
C. broken D. weak

But Charlotte had been practising without a licence. She had __14__ a doctor's licence in both Montreal and Winnipeg, but was __15__. The Manitoba College of Physicians and Surgeons, an all-male board, wanted her to __16__ her studies at a Canadian medical college! Charlotte refused to __17__ her patients to spend time studying what she already knew. So in 1887, she appealed to the Manitoba Legislature to __18__ a licence to her but they, too, refused. Charlotte __19__ to practise without a licence until 1912. She died four years later at the age of 73.

( ) 14. A. put away B. taken over
C. turned in D. applied for

( ) 15. A. punished B. refused
C. blamed D. fired

( ) 16. A. display B. change
C. preview D. complete

( ) 17. A. leave B. charge
C. test D. cure

( ) 18. A. sell B. donate
C. issue D. show

( ) 19. A. continued B. promised
C. pretended D. dreamed

In 1993, 77 years after her __20__, a medical licence was issued to Charlotte. This decision was made by the Manitoba Legislature to honor "this courageous and pioneering woman."【2014 大陸山東卷】

( ) 20. A. birth B. death
C. wedding D. graduation

Test 9 詳解

（2014 大陸山東卷）

Charlotte Whitehead was born *in England in 1843*, ***and*** moved to Montreal, Canada *at the age of five with her family.*

夏綠蒂‧懷特海於 1843 年出生在英國，她在五歲的時候跟著家人移居到加拿大的蒙特婁。

Charlotte Whitehead〔ˈʃɑrlət ˈhwaɪthɛd〕*n.* 夏綠蒂‧懷特海

Montreal〔ˌmɑntrɪˈɔl〕*n.* 蒙特婁【加拿大地名】

at the age of 在…歲的時候

be born in 出生於某地（某時）

be born into 出生於…的家庭

be born with 帶著…的能力出生

***While** nursing her ill elder sister for several years*, Charlotte discovered *she has an interest in medicine*.

（1 = nursing, 2 = interest）

當這些年照料她體弱多病的姐姐時，夏綠蒂發現她對醫學有興趣。

（1 = 照料, 2 = 興趣）

discover〔dɪˈskʌvɚ〕*v.* 發現

***While** nursing*…源自 ***While** she was nursing*…。

副詞子句中，句意很明顯時，主詞和 be 動詞可同時省略。

【詳見「文法寶典」p.645】

1. (**C**) 依句意，選 (C) ***nursing***。nurse〔 nɝs 〕*v.* 照顧
   而 (A) raise〔 rez 〕*v.* 養育，(B) 教導，
   (D) miss〔 mɪs 〕*v.* 思念，則不合句意。

2. (**B**) 依句意，選 (B) ***interest***「興趣」。
   have an interest in 對～有興趣
   而 (A) 習慣，(C) 意見，(D) voice〔 vɔɪs 〕*n.* 聲音；發言權，
   have a voice in「對～有發言權」，則不合句意。

At 18 she married and started (3) a family. Several years later, Charlotte said she wanted to be a doctor (4). Her husband supported her decision.

在 18 歲的時候她結婚了，而且開始有了 (3) 一個家庭。幾年後，夏綠蒂說她想要當醫生 (4)。她的丈夫也支持她的決定。

3. (**D**) 依句意，選 (D) ***started***「開始」。
   而 (A) invent *v.* 發明，(B) select *v.* 選擇，
   (C) offer〔ˈɔfɚ〕*v.* 提供，則不合句意。

4. (**A**) 依句意，選 (A) ***doctor***「醫生」。
   而 (B) 音樂家，(C) 律師，
   (D) physicist〔ˈfɪzəsɪst〕*n.* 物理學家，則不合句意。

Unfortunately, Canadian medical schools did not accept
5 6

women students *at the time*.

不幸的是，加拿大的醫學院在當時不接受女學生。
5 6

Canadian〔kə'nedɪən〕*adj.* 加拿大的

medical school 醫學院　***at the time*** 在當時（= *at that time*）

5.（**B**）依句意，選(B) ***Unfortunately***〔ʌn'fɔrtʃənɪtlɪ〕*adv.* 不幸地；遺憾地。(A) besides「此外」，(C) otherwise「否則」，(D) eventually〔ɪ'vɛntʃuəlɪ〕*adv.* 最後；終於，則不合句意。

6.（**D**）依句意，選(D) ***accept***「接受」。
而 (A) hire〔haɪr〕*v.* 雇用，
(B) entertain〔,ɛntə'ten〕*v.* 娛樂，
(C) trust *v.* 信任，則不合句意。

Therefore, Charlotte went to the United States *to study*

medicine at the Women's Medical College in Philadelphia. It
7

took her five years *to earn her medical degree.*
8

因此，夏綠蒂前往美國，在一家費城的女子醫學院研讀醫學。她花了五年的時間獲得她的醫學學位。
7 8

Philadelphia〔,fɪlə'dɛlfiə〕*n.* 費城【美國城市】
take〔tek〕*v.* 花費　　degree〔dɪ'gri〕*n.* 學位
It 爲虛主詞，代替眞正主詞 to earn…degree。

7.（**C**）依句意，選 (C) ***medicine***「醫學」。而 (A) 歷史，
(B) physics〔'fɪzɪks〕*n.* 物理學，(D) 法律，則不合句意。

8.（**D**）依句意，選 (D) ***earn***〔ɝn〕*v.* 獲得。
而 (A) improve〔ɪm'pruv〕*v.* 改善，(B) save〔sev〕*v.*
節省，(C) design〔dɪ'zaɪn〕*v.* 設計，則不合句意。

Upon graduation, Charlotte returned(9) to Montreal ***and*** set up a private clinic(10).

夏綠蒂一畢業就回到(9)蒙特婁，並且設立了一間私人診所(10)。

upon〔ə'pɑn〕*prep.* 一…就（= *on*）
graduation〔,grædʒʊ'eʃən〕*n.* 畢業　　***set up*** 設立
private〔'praɪvɪt〕*adj.* 私人的

9.（**A**）依句意，選 (A) ***returned***「返回」。
而 (B) escape〔ə'skep〕*v.* 逃走，(C) spread〔sprɛd〕*v.*
散播，(D) wander〔'wɑndɚ〕*v.* 徘徊；逗留，則不合句意。

10.（**C**）依句意，選 (C) ***clinic***〔'klɪnɪk〕*n.* 診所。而 (A) 學校，
(B) 博物館，(D) lab〔læb〕*n.* 實驗室（= *laboratory*），
則不合句意。

Three years later, she moved to Winnipeg, Manitoba, ***and*** *there* she was *once again* a busy doctor.
11

三年後，她移居到曼尼托巴的溫尼伯，而在那裡她依然是一個忙碌的醫生。
11

Winnipeg〔'wɪnə,pɛg〕*n.* 溫尼伯【加拿大地名】
Manitoba〔mænɪ'tobə〕*n.* 曼尼托巴【加拿大地名】
once again 再一次；依舊

11.（**A**）依句意，選 (A) ***busy***「忙碌的」。
而 (B) wealthy〔'wɛlθɪ〕*adj.* 有錢的，(C) greedy〔'gridɪ〕*adj.* 貪心的，(D) lucky「幸運的」，則不合句意。

Many *of her patients* were from the nearby timber ***and*** railway camps. Charlotte found herself operating *on damaged limbs*
12
and setting broken bones, [*in addition to delivering all the*
13
babies in the area.]

她的病人很多是來自附近的林場或是鐵路旁的工寮。夏綠蒂發現她除了
12
要對受傷的四肢動手術，以及接合斷掉的骨頭之外，她還要接生那個地區所有的嬰兒。
13

patient〔ˈpeʃənt〕*n.* 病人 nearby〔ˈnɪrˌbaɪ〕*adj.* 附近的

timber〔ˈtɪmbɚ〕*n.* 林場 operate〔ˈɑpeˌret〕*v.* 動手術

limbs〔lɪmbs〕*n. pl.* 四肢 set〔sɛt〕*v.* 接合（骨頭）

in addition to 除了…之外還有

deliver〔dɪˈlivɚ〕*v.* 接生

12.（**B**）依句意，選(B) ***found***「發現」。

(C) trouble〔ˈtrʌbḷ〕*v.* 使困擾

(D) imagine〔ɪˈmædʒɪn〕*v.* 想像

13.（**C**）依句意，選(C) ***broken***「斷掉的」。

(A) harmful〔ˈhɑrmfəl〕*adj.* 有害的

But Charlotte had been practising without a licence.

She had applied for (14) a doctor's licence *in both Montreal **and** Winnipeg*, ***but*** was refused (15).

但是夏綠蒂一直都是無照行醫。她曾在蒙特婁跟溫尼伯申請 (14) 過醫生執照，但都被拒絕 (15) 了。

practise〔ˈpræktɪs〕*v.* 執業（= *practice*）【***practise medicine*** 行醫】

licence〔ˈlaɪsṇs〕*n.* 執照

過去完成進行式 had been practising 敘述某動作從較早的過去繼續到過去某時，且強調該動作在過去某時還在繼續進行。

【詳見「文法寶典」p.349】

both A and B A 跟 B

14. (**D**) 依句意，選 (D) ***applied for***「申請」。
而 (A) put away「收拾」，(B) take over「接管」，
(C) turn in「繳交」，則不合句意。

15. (**B**) 依句意，選 (B) ***refused***「拒絕」。而 (A) 處罰，(C) blame
〔blem〕*v.* 責備，(D) fire *v.* 開除，則不合句意。

The Manitoba College of Physicians and Surgeons, *an all-male board*, wanted her to complete her studies *at a Canadian medical college*!
16

曼尼托巴內外科醫學院中，全由男性組成的委員會希望她能夠在加拿大的醫學院完成她的學業！
16

physician〔fə'zɪʃən〕*n.* 內科醫生
surgeon〔'sɝdʒən〕*n.* 外科醫生　male〔mel〕*n.* 男性
board〔bord〕*n.* 委員會　studies〔'stʌdɪz〕*n. pl.* 學業

16. (**D**) 依句意，選 (D) ***complete***〔kəm'plit〕*v.* 完成。
而 (A) display〔dɪ'sple〕*v.* 展示，
(C) preview〔'pri,vju〕*v.* 試演；試映，則不合句意。

Charlotte refused to leave her patients *to spend time studying* ***what*** *she already knew*.
17

夏綠蒂拒絕離開她的病患，去花時間學習她已經知道的東西。
17

「spend + 時間 + (in) + V-ing」表「花時間…」。

17. (**A**) 依句意，選 (A) ***leave***「離開」。
而 (B) charge〔tʃɑrdʒ〕*v.* 收費；控告，(C) 測試，
(D) cure〔kjʊr〕*v.* 治療，則不合句意。

So in 1887, she appealed to the Manitoba Legislature to issue (18) a licence *to her* but they, *too*, refused. Charlotte continued (19) to practise *without a licence until 1912*. She died four years later at the age of 73.

所以在 1887 年，她懇求曼尼托巴州議會發(18)執照給她，但他們也拒絕了。夏綠蒂繼續(19)無照執業直到 1912 年。她四年後去世，享年 73 歲。

appeal to 向…懇求（= *ask*）
legislature〔ˈlɛdʒɪsˌletʃɚ〕*n.* 立法機構；州議會

18. (**C**) 依句意，選 (C) ***issue***〔ˈɪʃʊ〕*v.* 發出。而 (A) 販賣，
(B) donate〔ˈdonet〕*v.* 捐贈，(C) show *v.* 顯示，
則不合句意。

19. (**A**) 依句意，選 (A) ***continued***「繼續」。
而 (B) promise〔ˈprɑmɪs〕*v.* 承諾，(C) pretend〔prɪˈtɛnd〕
v. 假裝，(D) dream *v.* 夢想，則不合句意。

In 1993, *77 years after her* <u>death</u>, a medical licence was
20
issued to Charlotte. This decision was made *by the Manitoba Legislature to honor* "*this courageous* ***and*** *pioneering woman.*"

在 1993 年，她<u>死</u>後的七十七年，醫師執照就發給了夏綠蒂。這個決定
20
是曼尼托巴州議會做的，要表揚「這位勇敢且具有開創性的女性」。

decision〔dɪ'sɪʒən〕*n.* 決定　　***make a decision*** 做決定
honor〔'ɑnɚ〕*v.* 表揚
courageous〔kə'redʒəs〕*adj.* 勇敢的（= *brave* = *bold* = *daring* = *heroic* = *valiant*〔'veljənt〕= *dauntless*〔'dɔntlɪs〕）
pioneering〔,paɪə'nɪrɪŋ〕*adj.* 有開創性的
pioneer〔,paɪə'nɪr〕當名詞用時爲「開拓者；先驅」，
當動詞用時爲「開創；率先（做⋯）」（= *initiate*〔ɪ'nɪʃɪ,et〕）。
【諧音：派二你兒，派出兩個你的兒子當先驅】

【例】This South African surgeon *pioneered* heart transplants.
（這位南非的外科醫生率先做了心臟移植。）

20.（**B**）依句意，選 (B) ***death***「死亡」。而 (A) 出生，
(C) wedding〔'wɛdɪŋ〕*n.* 婚禮，
(D) graduation〔,grædʒʊ'eʃən〕*n.* 畢業，則不合句意。

Test 10

Read the following passage and choose the best answer for each blank from the list below.

Parents feel that it is difficult to live with teenagers. Then again, teenagers have ___1___ feelings about their parents, saying that it is not easy living with them. According to a recent study, the most common ___2___ between parents and teenagers is that regarding untidiness and daily routine tasks. On the one hand, parents go mad over ___3___ rooms, clothes thrown on the floor and their children's refusal to help with the ___4___. On the other hand, teenagers lose their patience when parents continually blame them for ___5___ the towel in the bathroom, not cleaning up their room or refusing to do the shopping at the supermarket.

( ) 1. A. natural B. strong
C. guilty D. similar

( ) 2. A. interest B. argument
C. link D. knowledge

( ) 3. A. noisy B. crowded
C. messy D. locked

( ) 4. A. homework B. housework
C. problem D. research

( ) 5. A. washing B. using
C. dropping D. replacing

The research, conducted by St. George University, shows that different parents have different __6__ to these problems. However, some approaches are more __7__ than others. For example, those parents who yell at their children for their untidiness, but __8__ clean the room for them, have fewer chances of changing their children's __9__. On the contrary, those who let teenagers experience the ___10___ of their actions can do better. For example, when teenagers who don't help their parents with the shopping don't find their favorite drink in the refrigerator, they are forced to ___11___ their actions.

( ) 6. A. approaches B. contributions
C. introductions D. attitudes

( ) 7. A. complex B. popular
C. scientific D. successful

( ) 8. A. later B. deliberately
C. seldom D. thoroughly

( ) 9. A. behavior B. taste
C. future D. nature

( ) 10. A. failures B. changes
C. consequences D. thrills

( ) 11. A. defend B. delay
C. repeat D. reconsider

Psychologists say that ___12___ is the most important thing in parent-child relationships. Parents should ___13___ to their children, but at the same time they should lend an ear to what they have to say. Parents may ___14___ their children when they are untidy, but they should also understand that their room is their own private space. Communication is a two-way process. It is only by listening to and ___15___ each other that problems between parents and children can be settled.【2014 大陸廣東卷】

( ) 12. A. communication B. bond
C. friendship D. trust

( ) 13. A. reply B. attend
C. attach D. talk

( ) 14. A. hate B. scold
C. frighten D. stop

( ) 15. A. loving B. observing
C. understanding D. praising

Test 10 詳解

(2014 大陸廣東卷)

Parents feel ***that*** *it is difficult to live with teenagers. Then again*, teenagers have <u>similar</u> feeling *about their parents*, saying ***that*** *it is not easy living with them.*
1

父母都覺得與青少年一起生活是困難的。但話說回來，青少年對父母也有<u>相似的</u>感覺，他們說跟父母一起生活並不容易。
1

saying that…them 為分詞構句，其省略之主詞與前面的主詞必須相同，而動詞 say 為主動語態，故使用現在分詞。

teenager〔ˈtin,edʒɚ〕*n.* 青少年

1. (**D**) 依句意，選 (D) ***similar***「相似的」。而 (A) 自然的，(B) 強壯的，(C) guilty〔ˈgɪltɪ〕*adj.* 有罪的，則不合句意。

According to a recent study, the *most* common <u>argument</u> *between parents* ***and*** *teenagers* is that *regarding untidiness* ***and*** *daily routine tasks.*
2

依據一項最近的研究，親子間最常見的<u>爭吵</u>是關於不整潔及日常生活中的例行公事。
2

regarding 前的 that 爲 the most common argument 的代名詞。

recent〔ˈrisn̩t〕*adj.* 最近的　study〔ˈstʌdɪ〕*n.* 研究

common〔ˈkɑmən〕*adj.* 常見的

regarding〔rɪˈgɑrdɪŋ〕*prep.* 關於（= *concerning* = *respecting* = *about*）　untidiness〔ʌnˈtaɪdɪnɪs〕*n.* 不整潔

daily〔ˈdelɪ〕*adj.* 日常的　routine〔ruˈtin〕*adj.* 例行的

2.（**B**）依句意，選 (B) ***argument***「爭吵」。而 (A) 興趣，(C) link〔lɪŋk〕*n.* 連結，(D) 知識，則不合句意。

On the one hand, parents go mad *over messy rooms, clothes thrown on the floor* ***and*** *their children's refusal to help with the housework.*

一方面，父母會爲了凌亂的房間、丟在地板上的衣服，及孩子拒絕幫忙做家事而抓狂。

on the one hand「一方面」，而 ***on the other hand*** 則是指「另一方面」。

mad〔mæd〕*adj.* 生氣的　***go mad over*** 爲了…而抓狂

refusal〔rɪˈfjuzl̩〕*n.* 拒絕

3.（**C**）依句意，選 (C) ***messy***〔ˈmɛsɪ〕*adj.* 凌亂的。

而 (A) noisy〔ˈnɔɪzɪ〕*adj.* 吵鬧的，

(B) crowded〔ˈkraʊdɪd〕*adj.* 擁擠的，

(D) locked〔lɑkt〕*adj.* 鎖上的，則不合句意。

4. (**B**) 依句意，選 (B) ***housework***「家事」。

而 (A) homework「家庭作業」，(C) 問題，(D) 研究，

則不合句意。

On the other hand, teenagers lose their patience ***when*** *parents continually blame them for* dropping *the towel in the bathroom, not cleaning up their room* ***or*** *refusing to do the shopping at the supermarket.*

5

另一方面，當父母一再地爲了把毛巾掉在浴室、沒有將房間打掃乾淨，或是拒絕去超市買東西而指責青少年時，他們會失去耐心。

5

continually 通常表「持續地」，但是這裡作「往往；一再地」(= *repeatedly*) 解。

patience〔ˈpeʃəns〕*n.* 耐心　　blame〔blem〕*v.* 責備

towel〔ˈtaʊəl〕*n.* 毛巾　　***clean up*** 把…打掃乾淨

refuse〔rɪˈfjuz〕*v.* 拒絕　　***do the shopping*** 購物

5. (**C**) 依句意，選 (C) ***dropping***「使掉落」。而 (A) 洗，(B) 使用，(C) replace〔rɪˈples〕*v.* 取代，則不合句意。

The research, *conducted by St. George University*, shows ***that** different parents have different* <u>*approaches*</u> *to these problems.*
6

這個由聖喬治大學所做的研究顯示，不同的父母對這些問題有不同的<u>處理方式</u>。
6

conducted by St. George University 用來修飾主詞 The research。

conduct〔kən'dʌkt〕*v.* 進行；做

6.（**A**）依句意，選 (A) ***approaches***〔ə'protʃɪz〕*n. pl.* 處理方式（= *methods* = *ways* = *means*）。
而 (B) contribution〔ˌkɑntrə'bjuʃən〕*n.* 貢獻，
(C) introduction〔ˌɪntrə'dʌkʃən〕*n.* 介紹，
(D) attitude〔'ætəˌtjud〕*n.* 態度，則不合句意。

However, some approaches are *more* <u>successful</u> ***than*** other.
7

然而，有的方法比其他的方法來的<u>成功</u>。
7

7.（**D**）依句意，選 (D) ***successful***「成功的」。
而 (A) complex〔'kɑmplɛks〕*adj.* 複雜的，
(B) popular〔'pɑpjələ˞〕*adj.* 受歡迎的，
(C) scientific〔saɪ'tɪfɪk〕*adj.* 科學的，則不合句意。

For example, those parents ***who** yell at their children for their untidiness, **but** later clean the room for them*, have fewer chances *of changing their children's behavior*.

例如，那些爲了孩子不整潔而大罵的父母，若是罵完後幫他們清理房間，那改變孩子行爲的機會就會比較小。

who yell at their children…them 是形容詞子句，修飾 parents。
tidy 爲形容詞「整潔的」，其名詞爲 tidiness，un 表否定，故 untidiness 爲「不整潔；邋遢」。

8. (**A**) 依句意，選 (A) ***later***「之後」。
而 (B) deliberately〔dɪ'lɪbərɪtlɪ〕*adv.* 故意地，(C) 很少，(D) thoroughly〔'θɝolɪ〕*adv.* 徹底地，則不合句意。

9. (**A**) 依句意，選 (A) ***behavior***「行爲」(= *conduct*)。
而 (B) taste〔test〕*n.* 品味，(C) 未來，(D) nature〔'netʃɚ〕*n.* 本性，則不合句意。

On the contrary, those ***who** let teenagers experience the consequences of their actions* can do *better*.

相反地，那些讓青少年體驗他們行爲後果的父母，可能情況會比較好。
10

experience 原本爲名詞「經驗」，這裡是動詞，作「經歷；體驗」解。

on the contrary 相反地　　do〔du〕*v.* 進展；表現

10. (**C**) 依句意，選 (C) ***consequences***〔'kɑnsɪ,kwənsɪz〕*n. pl.* 後果。
而 (A) 失敗，(B) 改變，(D) thrill〔θrɪl〕*n.* 興奮；刺激，則不合句意。

For example, [***when*** *teenagers* ***who*** *don't help their parents with the shopping don't find their favorite drink in the refrigerator*], they are forced to reconsider their action.
11

例如，當不幫忙父母採買的青少年，在冰箱裡找不到他們最愛的飲料時，他們就被迫要重新思考自己的行爲。
11

drink〔drɪŋk〕*n.* 飲料　　refrigerator〔rɪ'frɪdʒə,retɚ〕*n.* 冰箱
force〔fors〕*v.* 強迫　　***be forced to V.*** 強迫～
action〔'ækʃən〕*n.* 行爲

11. (**D**) 依句意，選 (D) ***reconsider***〔,rikən'sidɚ〕*v.* 重新思考。
re (*again*) + consider (*v.*)
而 (A) defend〔dɪ'fɛnd〕*v.* 保衛，(B) delay〔dɪ'le〕*v.* 使延遲，(C) repeat〔rɪ'pit〕*v.* 重複，則不合句意。

Psychologists say ***that*** communication *is the most important thing in parent-child relationships*.
12

心理學家說，溝通是親子關係中最重要的事。
12

psychology（心理學）– y + ist（人）= psychologist，研究心理學的人，就是「心理學家」。

12.（**A**）依句意，選 (A) ***communication***〔,kəmjunə'keʃən〕*n.* 溝通。而 (B) bond〔bɑnd〕*n.* 連結，(C) 友誼，(D) 信任，則不合句意。

Parents should talk to their children, ***but*** *at the same time* they should lend an ear to ***what*** *they have to say*.
13

父母應該要和孩子說話，但同時他們應該要傾聽孩子要說的話。
13 13

lend a ear to 字面意思是「借一隻耳朵給…」，引申爲「傾聽」。
at the same time 同時

13.（**D**）依句意，選 (D) ***talk to***「和…說話」。
而 (A) reply〔rɪ'plaɪ〕*v.* 回答，
(B) attend〔ə'tɛnd〕*v.* 參加，attend to「照顧」，
(C) attach〔ə'tætʃ〕*v.* 附上；貼上，則不合句意。

Parents may scold their children ***when*** *they are untidy*, ***but***
14

they should *also* understand ***that*** *their room is their own private space.*

父母在孩子不整潔時可以責罵他們，但是也應了解，孩子的房間是他們的私人空間。
14

14. (**B**) 依句意，選 (B) ***scold*** [skold] *v.* 責罵。
而 (A) hate [het] *v.* 討厭，(C) frighten [ˈfraɪtn̩] *v.* 使驚嚇，(D) 阻止，則不合句意。

Communication is a two-way process. It is *only by listening to* ***and*** *understanding each other* ***that*** *problems between parents* ***and*** *children* can be settled.
15

溝通是雙向的過程。只有藉著傾聽、了解彼此，才能解決親子間的問題。
15

two-way *adj.* 雙向的　　process [ˈprɑsɛs] *n.* 過程
settle [ˈsɛtl̩] *v.* 解決

15. (**C**) 依句意，選 (C) ***understanding***「了解」。而 (A) 愛，(B) observe [əbˈzɝv] *n.* 觀察，(D) 稱讚，則不合句意。

Test 11

Read the following passage and choose the best answer for each blank from the list below.

As a general rule, all forms of activity lead to boredom when they are performed on a routine (常規) basis. As a matter of fact, we can see this __1__ at work in people of all __2__. For example, on Christmas morning, children are excited about __3__ with their new toys. But their __4__ soon wears off and by January those __5__ toys can be found put away in the basement.

( ) 1. A. principle B. habit
C. way D. power

( ) 2. A. parties B. races
C. countries D. ages

( ) 3. A. working B. living
C. playing D. going

( ) 4. A. confidence B. interest
C. anxiety D. sorrow

( ) 5. A. same B. extra
C. funny D. usual

The world is full of __6__ stamp albums and unfinished models, each standing as a monument to someone's __7__ interest. When parents bring home a pet, their child __8__ bathes it and brushes its fur. Within a short time, however, the __9__ of caring for the animal is handed over to the parents. Adolescents enter high school with great __10__ but are soon looking forward to __11__. The same is true of the young adults going to college.

( ) 6. A. well-organized
B. colorfully-printed
C. newly-collected
D. half-filled

( ) 7. A. broad B. passing
C. different D. main

( ) 8. A. silently B. impatiently
C. gladly D. worriedly

( ) 9. A. promise B. burden
C. right D. game

( ) 10. A. courage B. calmness
C. confusion D. excitement

( ) 11. A. graduation B. independence
C. responsibility D. success

And then, how many ___12___, who now complain（抱怨）about the long drives to work, ___13___ drove for hours at a time when they first ___14___ their driver's licenses（執照）? Before people retire, they usually ___15___ to do a lot of ___16___ things, which they never had ___17___ to do while working. But ___18___ after retirement, the golfing, the fishing, the reading and all of the other pastimes become as boring as the jobs they ___19___. And, like the child in January, they go searching for new ___20___.【2014 大陸全國新課標卷】

( ) 12. A. children B. students
C. adults D. retirees

( ) 13. A. carefully B. eagerly
C. nervously D. bravely

( ) 14. A. required B. obtained
C. noticed D. discovered

( ) 15. A. need B. learn
C. start D. plan

( ) 16. A. great B. strange
C. difficult D. correct

( ) 17. A. time B. money
C. skills D. knowledge

( ) 18. A. only B. well
C. even D. soon

( ) 19. A. lost B. chose
C. left D. broke

( ) 20. A. pets B. toys
C. friends D. colleagues

Test 11 詳解

（2014 大陸全國新課標卷）

As a general rule, all forms *of activity* lead to boredom **when** *they are performed on a routine basis*.

一般說來，當任何型態的活動，變成一種常規習慣時，都會變得無趣。

as a general rule 一般說來　　form〔fɔrm〕*n.* 形式
lead to 導致　　boredom〔ˈbordəm〕*n.* 無聊
perform〔pɚˈfɔrm〕*v.* 實行；做
routine〔ruˈtin〕*adj.* 例行的　　basis〔ˈbesɪs〕*n.* 基礎
on a routine basis 例行地；一成不變地（= *routinely*）

As a matter of fact, we can see this principle (1) *at work in people of all ages* (2).

事實上，我們能夠在各種年齡(2)層的人們身上，看到這個法則(1)。

as a matter of fact 事實上　　***at work*** 運作中；產生影響

1.（**A**）依句意，選 (A) ***principle***〔ˈprɪnsəpḷ〕*n.* 原則；準則。
而 (B) habit〔ˈhæbɪt〕*n.* 習慣，(C) 方式，(D) 力量，
則不合句意。

2. (**D**) 依句意，選 (D) ***ages***「年齡」。

而 (A) party〔ˈpɑrtɪ〕*n.* 黨派；派對，

(B) race〔res〕*n.* 種族，(C) 國家，則不合句意。

For example, *on Christmas morning*, children are excited

about playing *with their new toys*.
3

舉例來說，在耶誕節的早晨，孩子們迫不急待地想要玩他們的新玩具。
3

for example 舉例來說　excited〔ɪkˈsaɪtɪd〕*adj.* 興奮的

3. (**C**) 依句意，選 (C) ***playing***「玩」。

But their interest *soon* wears off and *by January* those
4

same toys can be found put away *in the basement*.
5

但他們對新玩具的興趣很快就消磨殆盡，而那些同樣的玩具到了一月
4　5

時，就會被發現收納在地下室裡。

wear off 消耗；磨損；逐漸消失　***put away*** 收拾

basement〔ˈbesmənt〕*n.* 地下室

4. (**B**) 依句意，選 (B) ***interest***〔ˈɪntrɪst〕*n.* 興趣。

而 (A) confidence〔ˈkɑnfədəns〕*n.* 信心，

(C) anxiety〔æŋ'zaɪətɪ〕*n.* 焦慮，

(D) sorrow〔'sɑro〕*n.* 悲傷，則不合句意。

5. (**A**) 依句意，選 (A) ***same***「同樣的」。

而 (B) extra〔'ɛkstrə〕*adj.* 額外的，

(C) funny〔'fʌnɪ〕*adj.* 好笑的，(D) 通常的，則不合句意。

The world is full of half-filled(6) stamp albums ***and*** unfinished models, *each standing as a monument to someone's passing(7) interest.*

這個世界裡充滿了集到一半的(6)集郵册，以及未完成的模型，它們每個都像是個紀念碑似的，象徵著某個人一時的(7)興趣。

6. (**D**) 依句意，選 (D) ***half-filled***「半滿的」，在此指「收集到一半的」。而 (A) well-organized「規劃良好的」，

(B) colorfully-printed「彩色印刷的」，

(C) newly-collected「新收集的」，則不合句意。

7. (**B**) 依句意，選 (B) ***passing***「一時的；短暫的」。

而 (A) broad〔brɔd〕*adj.* 寬廣的」，(C) 不同的，

(D) main〔men〕*adj.* 主要的，則不合句意。

When *parents bring home a pet*, their child gladly bathes it ***and*** brushes its fur.
8

當父母們帶寵物回家時，他們的孩子們會興高采烈地幫牠洗澡，替牠刷毛。
8

pet〔 pɛt 〕*n.* 寵物　bathe〔 beð 〕*v.* 給…洗澡
brush〔 brʌʃ 〕*v.* 刷　fur〔 fɝ 〕*n.* 毛皮

8. (**C**) 依句意，選 (C) ***gladly***〔ˈglædlɪ〕*adv.* 高興地。
而 (A) silently〔ˈsaɪləntlɪ〕*adv.* 沈默地，
(B) impatiently〔ɪmˈpeʃəntlɪ〕*adv.* 不耐煩地，
(D) worriedly〔ˈwɝɪdlɪ〕*adv.* 擔心地，則不合句意。

Within a short time, *however*, the burden *of caring for the animal* is handed over *to the parents*.
9

然而，在很短的時間內，照顧寵物的重擔就轉交到父母手中。
9

within〔 wɪðˈɪn 〕*prep.* 在…之內
care for 照顧　***hand over*** 交給

9. (**B**) 依句意，選 (B) ***burden***〔ˈbɝdn̩〕*n.* 負擔；重擔。
而 (A) promise〔ˈprɑmɪs〕*n.* 承諾，
(C) right〔 raɪt 〕*n.* 權利，(D) 遊戲，則不合句意。

Adolescents enter high school *with great* <u>*excitement*</u>, ***but*** are *soon* looking forward to <u>graduation</u>. The same is true of the young adults *going to college*.
10 11

青少年很<u>興奮</u>地進入高中就讀，但是很快就在期待<u>畢業</u>。同樣的情形也發生在要上大學的年輕人身上。
10 11

adolescent (ˌædḷˈɛsn̩t) *n.* 青少年　***look forward to*** 期待
be true of 適用於

10. (**D**) 依句意，選 (D) ***excitement*** (ɪkˈsaɪtmənt) *n.* 興奮。
with great excitement 非常興奮地
而 (A) courage (ˈkɝɪdʒ) *n.* 勇氣，
(B) calmness (ˈkɑmnɪs) *n.* 冷靜，
(C) confusion (kənˈfjuʒən) *n.* 困惑，則不合句意。

11. (**A**) 依句意，選 (A) ***graduation*** (ˌgrædʒuˈeʃən) *n.* 畢業。
而 (B) independence (ˌɪndɪˈpɛndəns) *n.* 獨立，
(C) responsibility (rɪˌspɑnsəˈbɪlətɪ) *n.* 責任，
(D) 成功，則不合句意。

And *then*, how many <u>adults</u>, ***who*** *now complain about the long drives to work*, <u>*eagerly*</u> drove *for hours at a time* ***when*** *they first* <u>*obtained*</u> *their driver's licenses*?
12 13 14

此外，有多少現在在抱怨上班的車程太長的成年人，在他們剛拿到駕照時，非常渴望想要一次開好幾小時的車？

12 14 13

and then 此外；而且；再說
complain (kəm'plen) *v.* 抱怨 < *about* >
drive (draɪv) *n.* 車程 ***at a time*** 一次
license ('laɪsn̩s) *n.* 執照 ***driver's license*** 駕照

12. (**C**) 依句意，選 (C) ***adults***「成人」。
(D) retiree (rɪˌtaɪ'ri) *n.* 退休者

13. (**B**) 依句意，選 (B) ***eagerly*** ('igɚlɪ) *adv.* 渴望地。
而 (A) 小心地，(C) nervously ('nɝvəslɪ) *adv.* 緊張地，
(D) bravely ('brevlɪ) *adv.* 勇敢地，則不合句意。

14. (**B**) 依句意，選 (B) ***obtain*** (əb'ten) *v.* 獲得。
而 (A) require (rɪ'kwaɪr) *v.* 需要，
(C) notice ('notɪs) *v.* 注意到，
(D) discover (dɪ'skʌvɚ) *v.* 發現，則不合句意。

***Before** people retire*, they *usually* plan to do a lot of great things, ***which** they never had* time *to do **while** working*.
15 16 17

此外，在人們退休之前，他們通常會規劃要做許多很棒的事情，這些事情在他們還在工作時是沒有時間做的。
15 16 17

15. (**D**) 依句意，選 (D) ***plan***「計畫」。

16. (**A**) 依句意，選 (A) ***great***「很棒的」。

17. (**A**) 依句意，選 (A) ***time***「時間」。(C) skill〔skɪl〕*n.* 技巧

But <u>*soon*</u> ***after retirement***, the golfing, the fishing, the reading
18
and all of the other pastimes become *as* boring ***as the jobs***
they <u>*left*</u>.
19

但退休後，<u>很快地</u>，打高爾夫球、釣魚、閱讀，以及所有其他的消遣活
18
動，就變得像他們先前所<u>辭掉</u>的工作一樣無聊。
19

golfing〔ˈgɑlfɪŋ〕*n.* 打高爾夫求　　fishing〔ˈfɪʃɪŋ〕*n.* 釣魚
pastime〔ˈpæstaɪm〕*n.* 消遣

18. (**D**) 依句意，選 (D) ***soon***「很快地」。

19. (**C**) 依句意，選 (C) ***left***「離開」。***leave the job*** 離職

And, *like the child in January*, they go searching for new <u>toys</u>.
20
接著，就像一月的孩子們一樣，他們會開始搜尋新的<u>玩具</u>。
20

20. (**B**) 依句意，選 (B) ***toys***「玩具」。

(D) colleague〔ˈkɑlig〕*n.* 同事

Test 12

Read the following passage and choose the best answer for each blank from the list below.

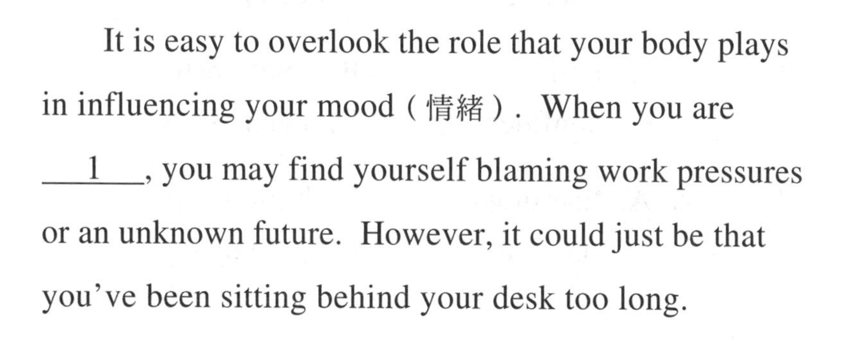

It is easy to overlook the role that your body plays in influencing your mood（情緒）. When you are ___1___, you may find yourself blaming work pressures or an unknown future. However, it could just be that you've been sitting behind your desk too long.

( ) 1. A. ill B. poor
C. unhappy D. unsuccessful

One way to improve your mood is ___2___. Psychologically, it provides you with a break from the stresses in your life. Also, in the process, you may aim for ___3___ goals, like a new personal running record or a better body shape. The achievement of a particular goal makes you feel good and contributes to your ___4___. That is why exercise is able to ___5___ your self-respect.

( ) 2. A. play B. communication
C. sleep D. exercise

( ) 3. A. clear B. present
C. common D. early

( ) 4. A. ability B. relationship
C. confidence D. business

( ) 5. A. tear down B. build up
C. set aside D. give up

You do not have to train yourself __6__ to feel the psychological benefits of exercise. What really matters is the __7__, not intensity (強度) of your exercise. You can try walking for 30 minutes five times per week or simply gardening on weekends.

【2013 大陸重慶卷】

( ) 6. A. hard B. everywhere
C. carefully D. late

( ) 7. A. time B. length
C. form D. frequency

Test 12 詳解

(2013 大陸重慶卷)

It is easy to overlook the role ***that*** *your body plays in influencing your mood.*

你很容易忽略你的身體在影響你的情緒中扮演的角色。

overlook〔'ovə,luk〕*v.* 忽略　role〔rol〕*n.* 角色
play〔ple〕*v.* 扮演　influence〔'ɪnfluəns〕*v.* 影響
mood〔mud〕*n.* 心情

When *you are unhappy*, you may find yourself blaming work pressures ***or*** an unknown future. *However*, it could *just* be ***that*** *you've been sitting behind your desk too long.*

當你身體不舒服的時候，你會發現你自己在責怪工作壓力或未知的未來。然而你可能只是坐在辦公桌前面太久了而已。

blame〔blem〕*v.* 責備　pressure〔'prɛʃə〕*n.* 壓力
unknown〔ʌn'non〕*adj.* 未知的

1. (**C**) 依句意，選 (C) ***unhappy***「不開心的」。
   而 (A) 生病的，(B) 窮的，(D) 不成功的，則不合句意。

One way to improve your mood is exercise.
2

有個能改善情緒的方法，那就是運動。
2

2. (**D**) 依句意，選 (D) ***exercise***「運動」。

(B) communication〔ˌkəmjunəˈkeʃən〕*n.* 溝通

Psychologically, it provides you *with a break from the stresses in your life*. *Also*, *in the process*, you may aim for clear goals, *like a new personal running record or a better body shape*.
3

從心理層面來說，運動能讓你休息一下，遠離生活中的壓力。此外，在這個過程中，你也可以設定清楚的目標，像是新的個人跑步紀錄，或是一個比較好的體態。
3

psychologically〔ˌsaɪkəˈlɑdʒɪkḷ〕*adv.* 心理上；從心理層面來說

provide sb. with sth. 提供某物給某人

stress〔strɛs〕*n.* 壓力 (= *pressure*)

process〔ˈprɑsɛs〕*n.* 程序　　***aim for*** 以…爲目標

body shape 體態

3. (**A**) 依句意，選 (A) ***clear***「清楚的」。

(B) present〔ˈprɛzṇt〕*adj.* 目前的

The achievement *of a particular goal* makes you feel good ***and*** contributes to your confidence.(4)

達成特定的目標，會讓你覺得很好，而且會有助於你的信心(4)。

achievement〔əˈtʃivmənt〕*v.* 成就；成就感
particular〔pɚˈtɪkjəlɚ〕*adj.* 特定的
contribute to 促成；有助於

4.(**C**) 依句意，選 (C) ***confidence***〔ˈkɑnfədəns〕*n.* 信心。
而 (A) ability「能力」，(B) relationship「關係」
(D) 生意，則不合句意。

That is ***why*** *exercise is able to build up your self-respect.*(5)

這就是爲什麼運動能建立(5)你的自尊心。

self-respect〔ˌsɛlfrɪˈspɛkt〕*n.* 自尊心

5.(**B**) 依句意，選 (B) ***build up***「增進；建立」（= *establish*）。
而 (A) tear down「拆除」（= *demolish*），
(C) set aside「擱置；保留」，
(D) give out「分發；送出」（= *distribute*），則不合句意。

You do not have to train yourself <u>*hard*</u> *to feel the*
6
psychological benefits of exercise. ***What*** *really matters* is
<u>frequency</u>, not intensity *of your exercise*.
7

你不必爲了感受運動對心理方面帶來的好處而<u>拼命</u>訓練自己。眞正
6
重要的，是你運動的<u>頻率</u>，而不是你運動的強度。
7

benefit〔'bɛnəfɪt〕*n.* 好處　　matter〔'mætɚ〕*v.* 重要
intensity〔ɪn'tɛnsətɪ〕*n.* 強度
複合關係代名詞 What 本身兼做先行詞跟關係代名詞，在此相當於 The thing that。【詳見「文法寶典」p.156】

6.（**A**）依句意，選 (A) ***hard***〔hɑrd〕*adv.* 拼命地；努力地。

7.（**D**）依句意，選 (D) ***frequency***「頻率」。

You can try walking *for 30 minutes five times per week* ***or*** *simply* gardening *on weekends*.
你可以試看看每週五次走路半小時，或是在週末時從事園藝。

time〔taɪm〕*n.* 次數　　per〔pɚ〕*prep.* 每…
garden〔'gɑrdn̩〕*v.* 從事園藝；栽培花木
weekend〔'wik'ɛnd〕*n.* 週末

Test 13

Read the following passage and choose the best answer for each blank from the list below.

Number sense is not the ability to count. It is the ability to recognize a ___1___ in number. Human beings are born with this ability. ___2___, experiments show that many animals are, too. For example, many birds have good number sense. If a nest has four eggs and you remove one, the bird will not ___3___. However, if you remove two, the bird ___4___ leaves. This means that the bird knows the ___5___ between two and three.

( ) 1. A. rise B. pattern C. change D. trend

( ) 2. A. Importantly B. Surprisingly C. Disappointedly D. Fortunately

( ) 3. A. survive B. find C. hatch D. notice

( ) 4. A. generally B. sincerely C. casually D. deliberately

( ) 5. A. distance B. range C. difference D. interval

Another interesting experiment showed a bird's ___6___ number sense. A man was trying to take a photo of a crow (烏鴉) that had a nest in a tower, but the crow always left when she saw him coming. The bird did not ___7___ until the man left the tower. The man had an ___8___. He took another man with him to the tower. One man left and the other stayed, but they did not ___9___ the bird. The crow stayed away until the second man left, too.

( ) 6. A. amazing B. annoying C. satisfying D. disturbing

( ) 7. A. relax B. recover C. react D. return

( ) 8. A. appointment B. excuse C. idea D. explanation

( ) 9. A. fool B. hurt C. catch D. kill

The experiment was ___10___ with three men and then with four men. But the crow did not return to the nest until all the men were ___11___. It was not until five men went into the tower and only four left that they were ___12___ able to fool the crow.

( ) 10. A. reported B. repeated
C. designed D. approved

( ) 11. A. confused B. gone
C. tired D. drunk

( ) 12. A. gradually B. luckily
C. strangely D. finally

How good is a human's number sense? It's not very good. For example, babies about fourteen months old almost always notice if something is taken away from a __13__ group. But when the number goes beyond three or four, the children are __14__ fooled.

( ) 13. A. single B. small C. local D. finally

( ) 14. A. seldom B. temporarily
C. merely D. often

It seems that number sense is something we have in common with many animals in this world, and that our human __15__ is not much better than a crow's.

【2013 大陸廣東卷】

( ) 15. A. sight B. nature C. ability D. belief

Test 13 詳解

(2013 大陸廣東卷)

Number sense is not the ability *to count*. It is the ability *to recognize a* change *in number*.
1

數字感並不是計算能力，而是指能察覺數目的變化的能力。
1

sense (sɛns) *n.* 感覺　***number sense*** 數字感
ability (əˈbɪlətɪ) *n.* 能力
able (能夠) + ility (*n.*)，就是「能力」(= *capability*)。
count (kaʊnt) *v.* 數；算　recognize (ˈrɛkəg,naɪz) *v.* 認出
number (ˈnʌmbɚ) *n.* 數字；數目

1. (**C**) 依句意，選 (C) ***change***「改變；變化」。
而 (A) rise (raɪz) *n.* 上升，(B) pattern (ˈpætɚn) *n.* 模式，(D) trend (trɛnd) *n.* 趨勢，則不合句意。

Human beings are born *with this ability*. Surprisingly,
2
experiments show ***that*** *many animals are*, *too*. *For example*, many birds have good number sense.

人類一生下來就有這個能力。令人驚訝的是，實驗顯示很多動物也有。
2
例如，很多鳥類都有不錯的數字感。

human beings 人類　***be born with*** 一出生就有
experiment〔ɪk'spɛrəmənt〕*n.* 實驗
that 引導名詞子句，做 show 的受詞。

2.（**B**）依句意，選 (B) ***surprisingly***「令人驚訝地」。
而 (A) importantly「重要地」，
(C) disappointedly「失望地」，
(D) fortunately「幸運地」，則不合句意。

***If** a nest has four eggs **and** you remove one*, the bird will not notice. 如果一個鳥巢有四顆蛋，而你拿走一顆，這隻鳥不會注意到。
3　3

3.（**D**）依句意，選 (D) ***notice***〔'notɪs〕*v.* 注意到。
而 (A) survive〔sə'vaɪv〕*v.* 存活，(B) find〔faɪnd〕*v.* 發現，(C) hatch〔hætʃ〕*v.* 孵化，則不合句意。

*However, **if** you remove two*, the bird generally leaves.
4
然而，如果你拿走了兩顆，這隻鳥就通常就會離開。
4

4.（**A**）依句意，選 (A) ***generally***「通常」。
而 (B) sincerely〔sɪn'sɪrlɪ〕*adv.* 眞誠地，
(C) casually〔'kæʒuəlɪ〕*adv.* 不在意地；簡便地，
(D) deliberately〔dɪ'lɪbərɪtlɪ〕*adv.* 故意地，則不合句意。

This means ***that*** *the bird knows the* <u>*difference*</u> *between two and three*. 這就代表這隻鳥知道二與三之間的<u>不同</u>。
5 5

5. (**C**) 依句意，選 (C) ***difference***「不同」。
而 (A) distance〔ˈdɪstəns〕*n.* 距離，
(B) range〔rændʒ〕*n.* 範圍，
(D) interval〔ˈɪntəvl̩〕*n.*（時間的）間隔，則不合句意。

Another interesting experiment showed a bird's <u>amazing</u> number sense. 另一個實驗也顯示出小鳥<u>很棒的</u>數字感。
6 6

6. (**A**) 依句意，選 (A) ***amazing***〔əˈmezɪŋ〕*adj.* 很棒的。
而 (B) annoying〔əˈnɔɪɪŋ〕*adj.* 令人心煩的，
(C) satisfying〔ˈsætɪs,faɪɪŋ〕*adj.* 令人滿意的，
(D) disturbing〔dɪˈstɝbɪŋ〕*adj.* 令人困擾的，則不合句意。

A man was trying to take a photo *of a crow* ***that*** *had a nest in a tower,* ***but*** the crow *always* left ***when*** *she saw him coming.* The bird did not <u>return</u> ***until*** *the man left the tower.*
7

有名男子想要拍一隻在塔上築巢的烏鴉，但烏鴉一看到他來的時候，就會離開。直到這名男子離開這座塔，這隻鳥才<u>回來</u>。
7

take a picture 拍照　crow〔 kro 〕*n.* 烏鴉

nest〔 nɛst 〕*n.* 巢　tower〔ˈtaʊɚ 〕*n.* 塔

not…until 直到～才…

7. (**D**) 依句意，選 (D) ***return***「回來」。

而 (A) relax〔 rɪˈlæks 〕*v.* 放鬆，

(B) recover〔 rɪˈkʌvɚ 〕*v.* 恢復，

(C) react〔 rɪˈækt 〕*v.* 反應，則不合句意。

The man had an idea. He took another man *with him to the tower*. 這名男士想到一個點子。他帶了另一名男子跟他去這座塔。
(8: idea / 點子)

8. (**C**) 依句意，選 (C) ***idea***「點子；想法」。

而 (A) appointment〔 əˈpɔɪntmənt 〕*n.* 約會，

(B) excuse〔 ɪkˈskjus 〕*n.* 藉口，

(D) explanation〔ˌɛkspləˈneʃən 〕*n.* 解釋，則不合句意。

One man left ***and*** the other stayed, ***but*** they did not fool the bird. 一位男子離開，而另一位留下來，但他們並沒有騙到這隻鳥。
(9: fool / 騙)

9. (**A**) 依句意，選 (A) ***fool***〔 ful 〕*v.* 欺騙。

而 (B) 傷害，(C) 抓到，(D) 殺死，則不合句意。

The crow stayed away ***until*** *the second man left, too.*
這隻烏鴉也仍然不回來，直到第二名男子離開。

The experiment was repeated (10) *with three men* ***and*** *then with four men.* ***But*** the crow did not return *to the nest* ***until*** *all the men were gone (11).*

這個實驗被以三個人和四個人重複進行(10)。但烏鴉仍然等到所有人都離開(11)才回來。

10.（**B**）依句意，選(B) ***repeated***「重複」。
而(A) 報導，(C) design〔dɪ'zaɪn〕*v.* 設計，
(D) approve〔ə'pruv〕*v.* 贊成，則不合句意。

11.（**B**）依句意，選(B) ***gone***〔gɔn〕*adj.* 離開的；消失的。
而(A) confused〔kən'fjuzd〕*adj.* 困惑的，(C) 疲倦的，
(D) 喝醉的，則不合句意。

It was ***not until*** *five men went into the tower* ***and*** *only four left* ***that*** *they were finally (12) able to fool the crow.*

一直到五名男子進去，而僅四名男子離開時，他們才終於(12)能夠騙過烏鴉。

It is/was not until…that~ 直到…才~　　***be able to V.*** 能夠…

12. (**D**) 依句意，選 (D) ***finally***「最後；終於」。
而 (A) gradually〔ˈɡrædʒʊəlɪ〕*adv.* 逐漸地，
(B) luckily〔ˈlʌkɪlɪ〕*n.* 幸運地，(C) 奇怪地，則不合句意。

How good is a human's number sense? It's not *very* good.
而人類的數字感有多好呢？其實沒有很好。

For example, babies *about fourteen months old almost always* notice ***if*** *something is taken away from a small group.*
13

例如，大約十四個月大的小嬰兒幾乎都會注意到是否有東西從一小堆東西中被拿走。
13

if 引導名詞子句，做 notice 的受詞。
group〔ɡrup〕*n.* 群體

13. (**B**) 依句意，選 (B) ***small***「小的」。
而 (A) single〔ˈsɪŋɡl̩〕*adj.* 單一的，
(C) local〔ˈlokl̩〕*adj.* 當地的，(D) 最後；終於，則不合句意。

But when *the number goes beyond three or four*, the children are *often* fooled.
14

但當數目超過三或四個的時候，小朋友常常會被騙。
14

14. (**D**) 依句意，選 (D) ***often***「常常」。而 (A) 很少，
(B) temporarily〔ˈtɛmpəˌrɛrəlɪ〕*adv.* 暫時地，
(C) merely〔ˈmɪrlɪ〕*adv.* 僅僅，則不合句意。

It seems ***that*** *number sense is something we have in common with many animals in this world*, and ***that*** *our human ability* (15) *is not much better* ***than*** *a crow's.*

這似乎在說明，數字感是我們與這世上許多動物的共同點，而人類的能力(15)並沒有比烏鴉的好多少。

It 爲形式主詞，that 子句才是眞正主詞。
have…in common 有…共同點

15. (**C**) 依句意，選 (C) ***ability***「能力」。
而 (A) sight〔saɪt〕*n.* 視力，
(B) nature〔ˈnetʃɚ〕*n.* 本質，
(D) belief〔bɪˈlif〕*n.* 信念；信仰，則不合句意。

Test 14

Read the following passage and choose the best answer for each blank from the list below.

Over the past few decades, more and more countries have opened up their markets, increasingly transforming the world economy into one free-flowing global market. The question is: Is economic globalization __1__ for all?

( ) 1. A. possible B. smooth
C. good D. easy

According to the World Bank, one of its chief supporters, economic globalization has helped reduce __2__ in a large number of developing countries. It quotes one study that shows increased wealth __3__ to improved education and longer life in twenty-four developing countries as a result of integration（融合）of local economies into the world economy. Home to some three billion people, these twenty-four countries have seen incomes __4__ at an average rate of five percent —compared to two percent in developed countries.

( ) 2. A. crime B. poverty
C. conflict D. population

( ) 3. A. contributing B. responding
C. turning D. owing

( ) 4. A. remain B. drop
C. shift D. increase

Those who ___5___ globalization claim that economies in developing countries will benefit from new opportunities for small and home-based businesses. ___6___, small farmers in Brazil who produce nuts that would originally have sold only in ___7___ open-air markets can now promote their goods worldwide by the Internet.

( ) 5. A. doubt B. define
C. advocate D. ignore

( ) 6. A. In addition B. For instance
C. In other words D. All in all

( ) 7. A. mature B. new
C. local D. foreign

Critics take a different view, believing that economic globalization is actually ___8___ the gap between the rich and poor. A study carried out by the U. N.-sponsored World Commission on the Social Dimension of Globalization shows that only a few developing countries have actually ___9___ from integration into the world economy and that the poor, the uneducated, unskilled workers, and native peoples have been left behind. ___10___, they maintain that globalization may eventually threaten emerging businesses.

( ) 8. A. finding B. exploring
C. bridging D. widening

( ) 9. A. suffered B. profited
C. learned D. withdrawn

( ) 10. A. Furthermore B. Therefore
C. However D. Otherwise

For example, Indian craftsmen who currently seem to benefit from globalization because they are able to ___11___ their products may soon face fierce competition that could put them out of __12__. When large-scale manufacturers start to produce the same goods, or when superstores like Wal-Mart move in, these small businesses will not be able to __13__ and will be crowded out.

( ) 11. A. consume B. deliver
C. export D. advertise

( ) 12. A. trouble B. business
C. power D. mind

( ) 13. A. keep up B. come in
C. go around D. help out

One thing is certain about globalization—there is no __14__. Advances in technology combined with more open policies have already created an interconnected world. The __15__ now is finding a way to create a kind of globalization that works for the benefit of all.

【2013 大陆上海卷】

( ) 14. A. taking off B. getting along
C. holding out D. turning back

( ) 15. A. agreement B. prediction
C. outcome D. challenge

Test 14 詳解

(2013 大陸上海卷)

Over the past few decades, more and more countries have opened up their markets, *increasingly* transforming the world economy *into one free-flowing global market.*

在過去的幾十年中，越來越多國家已經開放他們市場，世界經濟正逐漸轉變成一個自由流動的全球市場。

decade ('dɛked) *n.* 十年
increasingly (ɪn'krisɪŋlɪ) *adv.* 逐漸地
transform (træns'fɔrm) *v.* 使轉變
economy (ɪ'kɑnəmɪ) *n.* 經濟　　global ('globḷ) *adj.* 全球的

free-flowing *adj.* 自由流動的爲複合形容詞，形容詞 + 現在分詞，例如：a good-looking girl「好看的女孩」；an easy-going person「隨和的人」。

The question is: Is economic globalization <u>good</u> *for all*?
1

現在的問題是：經濟全球化對所有人都<u>好</u>嗎？
1

1. (**C**) 依句意，選 (C) ***good***。而 (A) 可能的，(B) smooth (smuθ) *adj.* 平滑的，(D) 容易的，則不合句意。

According to the World Bank, one of its chief supporters, economic globalization has helped reduce <u>poverty</u> *in a large number of developing countries.*
2

根據經濟全球化主要支持者之一的世界銀行說法，經濟全球化有助於降低許多開發中國家的<u>貧困</u>狀況。
2

World Bank 世界銀行【是為開發中國家資本項目提供貸款的聯合國（United Nations）國際金融機構。它是世界銀行集團的組成機構之一，也是聯合國發展集團的成員。世界銀行的官方目標為消除貧困】

chief〔tʃif〕*adj.* 主要的　economic〔ˌikəˈnɑmɪk〕*adj.* 經濟的

globalization〔ˌglobḷaɪˈzeʃən〕*n.* 全球化

a large number of 很多的

developing〔dɪˈvɛləpɪŋ〕*adj.* 開發中的

2.（**B**）依句意，選 (B) ***poverty***〔ˈpʌvətɪ〕*n.* 貧困；貧窮。
而 (A) crime *n.* 罪，(C) conflict〔ˈkɑnflɪkt〕*n.* 衝突，
(D) population *n.* 人口，則不合句意。

It quotes one study *__that__ shows increased wealth <u>contributing</u> to improved education __and__ longer life in twenty-four developing countries as a result of integration of local economies into the world economy.*
3

它引用了一項研究，研究指出，由於地方經濟整合入世界經濟，二十四個開發中國家財富的增加，有助於(3)改善教育，並讓人們有較長的壽命。

quote〔kwot〕*v.* 引用　***as a result of*** 因爲；由於
integration〔ˌɪntəˈgreʃən〕*n.* 整合
local〔ˈlokḷ〕*adj.* 當地的；地方的

3.（**A**）依句意，選(A) ***contributing***。
contribute to 促成；有助於；導致
而(B) respond〔rɪˈspɑnd〕*v.* 同意；反應 < *to* >，(C) turn to「向～求助」，(D) owing to「由於」，則不合句意。

Home to some three billion people, these twenty-four countries have seen incomes increase(4) *at an average rate of five percent—compared to two percent in developed countries.*
這些大約有三十億人的二十四個國家，收入已經平均增加(4)了百分之五—相較於已開發國家的百分之二。

be home to 是…的所在地　some〔sʌm〕*adv.* 大約
billion〔ˈbɪljən〕*n.* 十億　see〔si〕*v.* 經歷
rate〔ret〕*n.* 比率　***compared to*** 和～相比

4.（**D**）依句意，選(D) ***increase***〔ɪnˈkris〕*v.* 增加。
而(A) remain *v.* 仍然，(B) drop *v.* 減少，(C) shift〔ʃɪft〕*v.* 轉變，則不合句意。

Those ***who*** *advocate globalization* claim ***that*** *economies*
5

in developing countries will benefit from new opportunities

for small ***and*** *home-based businesses.*

那些擁護全球化的人聲稱，開發中國家的經濟，將從全球化帶給小
5
型企業和家庭公司的企業的新契機而獲益。

claim〔klem〕*v.* 宣稱　***benefit from*** 從…受益

home-based *adj.* 以家庭爲基礎的

home-based business 住家公司

5. (**C**) ad | voc | ate　從字首字根分析，advocate 意思是「強力
to | call | *v.*　呼喊」，就是「擁護；主張；倡導」。

依句意，選 (C)。

而 (A) doubt *v.* 懷疑，(B) define〔dɪ'faɪn〕*v.* 下定義，
(D) ignore〔ɪg'nor〕*v.* 忽視，則不合句意。

For instance, small farmers *in Brazil* ***who*** *produce nuts* ***that***
6

would originally have sold only in local open-air markets can
7

now promote their goods *worldwide by the Internet*.

例如，在巴西生產堅果小農戶，原本只在當地露天市場賣堅果，現在可以通過網路宣傳自己的商品。
(例如 6；當地 7)

Brazil〔brə'zɪl〕*n.* 巴西　nuts〔nʌts〕*n. pl.* 堅果
originally〔ə'rɪdʒɪnḷɪ〕*adv.* 原本　open-air *adj.* 露天的
promote〔prə'mot〕*v.* 促銷；宣傳　goods〔gʊdz〕*n. pl.* 商品

6.（**B**）依句意，選 (B) ***For instance*** 例如（= *For example*）。
而 (A) in addition「此外」，(C) in other words「換句話說」，(D) all in all「總之」，則不合句意。

7.（**C**）依句意，選 (C) ***local***〔'lokḷ〕*adj.* 當地的；本地的。
而 (A) mature〔mə'tʃʊr〕*adj.* 成熟的，(B) 新的，
(D) foreign〔'fɔrɪn〕*adj.* 外國的，則不合句意。

Critics take a different view, believing ***that*** *economic globalization is actually widening the gap between the rich and poor.*
(widening 8)

評論家持不同的看法，認爲經濟全球化實際上是擴大了貧富之間的差距。
(擴大 8)

critic〔'krɪtɪk〕*n.* 批評家；評論家
take a…view 抱持…看法（= *have a…opinion*）
actually〔'æktʃʊəlɪ〕*adv.* 事實上　gap〔gæp〕*n.* 差距

8.（**D**）依句意，選 (D) ***widening***。
widen〔'waɪdn̩〕*v.* 擴大；放寬；加寬

而 (A) find *v.* 找到，(B) explore〔ɪk'splor〕*v.* 探索，

(C) bridge〔brɪdʒ〕*v.* 消除（隔閡、差距），則不合句意。

A study *carried out by the U. N.-sponsored World Commission on the Social Dimension of Globalization* shows ***that*** *only a few developing countries have actually* *profited* (9) *from integration into the world economy* ***and that*** *the poor, the uneducated, unskilled workers,* ***and*** *native peoples have been left behind.*

一項由聯合國贊助的「國際全球化社會面向委員會」執行的研究指出，只有一些開發中國家，眞的從世界經濟整合中獲益 (9)，而窮人、沒有受過教育的人、沒有技術的勞工，以及原住民，則已經被遺忘。

carry out 執行（= *conduct*）

the U.N. 聯合國（= *the United Nations*）

sponsor〔'spɑnsɚ〕*v.* 贊助

dimension〔də'mɛnʃən〕*n.* 層面；方面

World Commission on the Social Dimension of Globalization

國際全球化社會面向委員會

unskilled〔ʌn'skɪld〕*adj.* 無技能的；不熟練的

native〔'netɪv〕*adj.* 土著的　　people〔'pipḷ〕*n.* 民族

leave behind 留下；遺忘

9. (**B**) 依句意，選 (B) ***profited***。profit [ˈprɑfit] *v.* 獲益
而 (A) suffer [ˈsʌfɚ] *v.* 受苦，(C) 學習，
(D) withdraw [wɪθˈdrɔ] *v.* 縮回；撤退，則不合句意。

Furthermore, they maintain ***that*** *globalization may eventually threaten emerging businesses.*
10

此外，他們認爲，全球化可能最終會威脅到新興企業。
10

maintain [menˈten] *v.* 堅稱；斷言

10. (**A**) 依句意，選 (A) ***Furthermore*** *adv.* 此外 (= *additionally* = *moreover* = *in addition*)。
而 (B) Therefore *adv.* 因此，(C) However *adv.* 然而，
(D) Otherwise *adv.* 否則，則不合句意。

For example, Indian craftsmen [***who*** *currently seem to benefit from globalization* ***because*** *they are able to export their products*] may *soon* face fierce competition ***that*** *could put them out of business.*
11 (export)　12 (business)

例如，因爲能夠<u>出口</u>產品，所以目前似乎能從全球化中受益的那些印度
11
工匠，可能很快就會面臨可能會讓他們歇<u>業</u>的激烈競爭。
12

craftsman〔ˈkræftsmən〕*n.* 工匠
currently〔ˈkɝəntlɪ〕*adv.* 目前　　fierce〔fɪrs〕*adj.* 激烈的
put〔pʊt〕*v.* 使受到；使遭遇

11. (**C**) 依句意，選 (C) ***export***〔ɪksˈport〕*v.* 輸出；出口。

12. (**B**) 依句意，選 (B) ***business*** *n.* 生意；交易。
out of business 歇業；停業；倒閉
而 (A) trouble *n.* 麻煩，
(C) power〔ˈpaʊɚ〕*n.* 力量；權力，
(D) mind〔maɪnd〕*n.* 心智；想法，則不合句意。

When *large-scale manufacturers start to produce the same goods*, ***or when*** *superstores like Wal-Mart move in*, these small businesses will not be able to <u>keep up</u> ***and*** will be crowded out.
13

當大型製造商開始生產相同的商品，或是當像沃爾瑪一樣的大型超市進駐，這些小企業將無法<u>保持</u>相同水準，而將被晾在一邊。
13

scale〔skel〕*n.* 規模
manufacturer〔ˌmænjʊˈfæktʃərɚ〕*n.* 製造商
superstore〔ˈsupɚˌstor〕*n.* 大型商場；大型超市
move in 搬進；遷入
crowd out 排擠（某人或某事物）（= *force out*）

13.（**A**）依句意，選 (A) ***keep up***「保持（同一速度或水準）；繼續」。
而 (B) come in「進來」，(C) go around「四處走動」，
(D) help out「幫助（某人）完成」，則不合句意。

One thing is certain *about globalization*—there is no turning back. Advances *in technology* combined with more open policies have *already* created an interconnected world.
14

關於全球化，有一件事是確定的—沒有回頭路。科技的進步結合更開放的政策，已經創造了一個相互連結的世界。
14

advance〔ədˈvæns〕*n.* 進步　　combine〔kəmˈbaɪn〕*v.* 結合
interconnected〔ˌɪntɚkəˈnɛktɪd〕*adj.* 互相連接的

14.（**D**）依句意，選 (D) ***turning back***「回頭路」。
turning back 源自於 ***turn back*** 此動詞片語，字面意思是「往回走」，引申為「折回；調轉頭」（= *return*）。
而 (A) take off「起飛」，(B) get along「進展」，
(C) hold out「伸出（手）」，則不合句意。

The challenge *now* is finding a way *to create a kind of*
15

globalization ***that*** *works for the benefit of all.*

現在的挑戰是要找到方法，來創造一種對所有人都有利的全球化。
15

create〔krɪ'et〕*v.* 創造　　work〔wɝk〕*v.* 運作；行得通

benefit〔'bɛnəfɪt〕*n.* 好處；益處

for the benefit of 爲了…的利益

bene ¦ fit 做得好，就會對別人有「好處；益處」。
well ¦ do

benefit 當動詞用爲「有益於；受益」。

【例】 Fresh air will *benefit* you.

（新鮮空氣有益於你的健康。）

【例】 Both sides have *benefited* from the talks.

（雙方都從談判中受益。）

that 爲「關係代名詞」，代替先行詞 globalization（全球化），引導形容詞子句。

15.（**D**）依句意，選 (D) ***challenge***〔'tʃælɪndʒ〕*n.* 挑戰。

而 (A) agreement〔ə'grimənt〕*n.* 協議，

(B) prediction〔prɪ'dɪkʃən〕*n.* 預測，

(C) outcome〔'aʊt,kʌm〕*n.* 結果，則不合句意。

Test 15

Read the following passage and choose the best answer for each blank from the list below.

Body language is the quiet, secret and most powerful language of all! It speaks ___1___ than words. According to specialists, our bodies send out more ___2___ than we realize. In fact, non-verbal（非言語）communication makes up about 50% of what we really ___3___. And body language is particularly ___4___ when we attempt to communicate across cultures. Indeed, what is called body language is so ___5___ a part of us that it's actually often unnoticed. And misunderstandings occur as a result of it.

(　) 1. A. straighter　　B. louder
　　　　C. harder　　D. further

(　) 2. A. sounds　　B. invitations
　　　　C. feelings　　D. messages

(　) 3. A. hope　　B. receive
　　　　C. discover　　D. convey

( ) 4. A. immediate B. misleading
C. important D. difficult

( ) 5. A. well B. far
C. much D. long

__6__, different societies treat the __7__ between people differently. Northern Europeans usually do not like having __8__ contact (接觸) even with friends, and certainly not with __9__. People from Latin American countries, __10__, touch each other quite a lot. Therefore, it's possible that in __11__, it may look like a Latino is __12__ a Norwegian all over the room. The Latino, trying to express friendship, will keep moving __13__. The Norwegian, very probably seeing this as pushiness, will keep __14__—which the Latino will in return regard as __15__.

( ) 6. A. For example B. Thus
C. However D. In short

(　) 7.	A. trade	B. distance
	C. connections	D. greetings
(　) 8.	A. eye	B. verbal
	C. bodily	D. telephone
(　) 9.	A. strangers	B. relatives
	C. neighbours	D. enemies
(　) 10.	A. in other words	B. on the other hand
	C. in a similar way	D. by all means
(　) 11.	A. trouble	B. conversation
	C. silence	D. experiment
(　) 12.	A. disturbing	B. helping
	C. guiding	D. following
(　) 13.	A. closer	B. faster
	C. in	D. away
(　) 14.	A. stepping forward	B. going on
	C. backing away	D. coming out
(　) 15.	A. weakness	B. carelessness
	C. friendliness	D. coldness

Clearly, a great deal is going on when people __16__. And only a part of it is in the words themselves. And when parties are from __17__ cultures, there's a strong possibility of __18__. But whatever the situation, the best __19__ is to obey the Golden Rule: treat others as you would like to be __20__.【2012 大陸全國新課標卷】

( ) 16. A. talk B. travel
C. laugh D. think

( ) 17. A. different B. European
C. Latino D. rich

( ) 18. A. curiosity B. excitement
C. misunderstanding D. nervousness

( ) 19. A. chance B. time
C. result D. advice

( ) 20. A. noticed B. treated
C. respected D. pleased

Test 15 詳解

(2012 大陸全國新課標卷)

Body language is the quiet, secret ***and*** *most* powerful language *of all*! It speaks louder[1] than words.

肢體語言是安靜、祕密，且最爲強而有力的語言！它的表達卻比話語來的強烈[1]。

body language 肢體語言　　secret〔ˈsikrɪt〕*adj.* 祕密的
powerful〔ˈpauəfəl〕*adj.* 強而有力的

1.(**B**) 依句意，選 (B) ***louder***〔ˈlaudɚ〕*adv.* 較大聲地。
而 (A) straighter〔ˈstretɚ〕*adv.* 較直地，
(C) harder〔ˈhɑrdɚ〕*adv.* 更努力地，
(D) further〔ˈfɝðɚ〕*adv.* 更進一步地，則不合句意。

According to specialists, our bodies send out *more* messages[2] ***than*** *we realize*.
根據專家的說法，我們的肢體傳達出來的訊息[2]，比我們所意識到的還要多。

specialist〔ˈspɛʃəlɪst〕*n.* 專家　　***send out*** 發出
realize〔ˈriəˌlaɪz〕*v.* 知道；了解

2. (**D**) 依句意，選 (D) ***messages*** 〔ˈmɛsɪdʒɪz〕*n. pl.* 訊息。

而 (A) 聲音，(B) invitation 〔ˌɪnvəˈteʃən〕*n.* 邀請，

(C) 感情，則不合句意。

In fact, non-verbal communication makes up about 50% *of* ***what*** *we really* convey.
3

事實上，非語言溝通組成了我們眞正傳達的百分之五十。
3

non-verbal 〔ˈnɑnˈvɝbl̩〕*n.* 非語言的　***make up*** 組成

3. (**D**) 依句意，選 (D) ***convey*** 〔kənˈve〕*v.* 傳達。

而 (A) 希望，(B) 接受，(C) 發現，則不合句意。

And body language is *particularly* important ***when*** *we attempt to communicate across cultures*.
4

而在我們企圖進行跨文化溝通時，肢體語言是格外重要的。
4

attempt 〔əˈtɛmpt〕*v.* 企圖；打算

4. (**C**) 依句意，選 (C) ***important*** *adj.* 重要的 (= *significant*)。

而 (A) immediate 〔ɪˈmidɪɪt〕*adj.* 立刻的，

(B) misleading 〔mɪsˈlidɪŋ〕*adj.* 誤導的，

(D) 困難的，則不合句意。

Indeed, ***what*** *is called body language* is ***so*** much a part *of us*
5

that *it's actually often unnoticed.*

確實，這稱作肢體語言的東西佔了我們很大的一部分，所以它實際上經常被忽略。
5

indeed〔ɪn'did〕*adv.* 的確　　***what is called*** 所謂的

actually〔'æktʃʊəlɪ〕*adv.* 事實上

unnoticed〔ʌn'notɪst〕*adj.* 未被發覺的；不被注意的

5.（**C**）依句意，選 (C) ***much***「多的；大量的」。

And misunderstandings occur *as a result of it*. *For example*, different societies treat the distance *between people differently*.
6 7

所以這樣的結果就是產生誤會。例如，不同社會看待人與人之間的距離是不同的。
6 7

6.（**A**）依句意，選 (A) ***For example***「例如」。而 (B) thus〔ðʌs〕*adv.* 因此，(C) 然而，(D) in short「簡言之」，則不合句意。

7.（**B**）依句意，選 (B) ***distance***〔'dɪstəns〕*n.* 距離。

而 (A) trade〔tred〕*n.* 貿易，

(C) connections〔kə'nɛkʃənz〕*n. pl.* 人際關係，

(D) greetings〔'gritɪŋz〕*n. pl.* 問候語；祝賀，則不合句意。

Northern Europeans *usually* do not like having bodily contact
8
even with friends, **and** *certainly not with strangers*.
9

北歐人通常不喜歡有身體上的接觸，即使是朋友也不例外，陌生人更不用說了。

本句中，bodily「身體上的」爲形容詞。

certain 中的 cert 字根是「證明、確定」的意思，例如：

certain *adj.* 確定的、certify *v.* 證明、certificate *n.* 證明書、ascertain *v.* 證實、certitude *v.* 確信等。

8. (**C**) 依句意，選 (C) ***bodily*** ('badılı) *adj.* 身體上的。

而 (B) verbal ('vɝbḷ) *adj.* 言辭上的；口頭的，則不合句意。

9. (**A**) 依句意，選 (A) ***stranger*** *n.* 陌生人。

而 (B) 親戚，(C) 鄰居，(D) 敵人，則不合句意。

People *from Latin American countries*, on the other hand,
10
touch each other *quite a lot*.

從另一方面來看，來自拉丁美洲的人，則是經常會碰觸彼此。
10

本句中，from 引導介系詞片語，修飾 People。

Latin American 拉丁美洲的；中南美洲的 ***a lot*** 常常

10. (**B**) 依句意，選 (B) ***on the other hand***「另一方面」。

而 (A) in other words「換句話說」，

(C) in a similar way「以類似的方式」，

(D) by all means「必定；一定；當然可以」，則不合句意。

Therefore, it's possible ***that*** *in* *conversation*, *it may look like* *a Latino is* *following* *a Norwegian all over the room.*

(11: conversation; 12: following)

因此，在對話時，場面可能看起來很像拉丁美洲人正跟著挪威人在房間裡到處走。

(11: 對話; 12: 跟著)

本句中眞正的主詞爲 that 所引導的名詞子句，it 爲虛主詞。

Latino〔 lə'tino 〕*n.* 拉丁美洲人

Norwegian〔 nɔr'widʒən 〕*n.* 挪威人

11. (**B**) 依句意，選 (B) ***conversation***「對話」。而 (A) 麻煩，

(C) silence〔'saɪləns 〕*n.* 安靜；沈默，(D) 實驗，則不合句意。

12. (**D**) 依句意，選 (D) ***following***「跟著」。

而 (A) disturb〔 dɪ'stɝb 〕*v.* 打擾，

(C) guide〔 gaɪd 〕*v.* 引導，則不合句意。

The Latino, *trying to express friendship*, will keep moving *closer*.

(13: closer)

這個想要表達友誼的拉丁美洲人，會不斷地靠近。
13

trying to express friendship 是形容詞子句簡化而來的分詞片語，省略了關代 who，且將動詞 try 改成現在分詞 + trying。

13. (**A**) 依句意，選 (A) ***closer***「更靠近」。
close〔klos〕*adv.* 接近地；靠近地

The Norwegian, *very probably seeing this as pushiness*, will keep backing away—***which*** *the Latino will in return regard as* coldness.
14 15

這位挪威人很可會認爲這是在不斷糾纏，而持續退後—這樣一來，拉丁美洲人則反過來認爲挪威人很冷漠。
14 15

see A as B 認爲 A 是 B　　pushiness〔ˈpuʃɪnɪs〕*n.* 糾纏不休

14. (**C**) 依句意，選 (C) ***backing away***「後退」。
而 (A) step forward「往前走」，(B) go on「繼續」，
(D) come out「出來」，則不合句意。

15. (**D**) 依句意，選 (D) ***coldness***「冷漠」。
而 (A) weakness *n.* 弱點；缺點，
(B) carelessness *n.* 粗心，
(C) friendliness「友善」，則不合句意。

Clearly, a great deal is going on ***when*** *people talk* (16). ***And*** only a part *of it* is in the words themselves.

顯而易見地，當人們說話(16)時，同時有很多事一起發生，話語的內容只是其中的一小部分而已。

a great deal 很多　***go on*** 發生（= *happen*）

word〔 wɝd 〕*n.* 話語

16.（**A**）依句意，選 (A) ***talk***「說話」。

And when *parties are from different* (17) *cultures*, there's a strong possibility *of misunderstanding* (18).

因此當一群人都來自不同的(17)文化時，就非常有可能會造成誤會(18)。

party〔ˈpɑrtɪ〕*n.* 一行人　possibility〔ˌpɑsəˈbɪlətɪ〕*n.* 可能性

17.（**A**）依句意，選 (A) ***different***「不同的」。而 (B) European〔ˌjurəˈpiən〕*adj.* 歐洲的，(C) Latino〔læˈtino〕*adj.* 拉丁美洲的，(D) 有錢的，則不合句意。

18.（**C**）依句意，選 (C) ***misunderstanding***〔mɪsˌʌndɚˈstændɪŋ〕*n.* 誤會。而 (A) curiosity〔ˌkjurɪˈɑsətɪ〕*n.* 好奇心，(B) excitement〔ɪkˈsaɪtmənt〕*n.* 刺激；興奮，(D) nervousness〔ˈnɝvəsnɪs〕*n.* 緊張，則不合句意。

***But whatever** the situation*, the best <u>advice</u> is to obey the
19

Golden Rule: treat others ***as** you would like to be <u>treated</u>.*
20

但是不管情況怎麼樣，最好的<u>建議</u>就是要遵守這一個金科玉律：以你所
19

希望被<u>對待</u>的方式來對待別人。
20

whatever〔hwɑtˈɛvɚ〕*adj.* 任何…的；無論什麼的

obey〔əˈbe〕*v.* 遵守

Golden Rule 金科玉律（= *golden rule*）

treat〔trit〕*v.* 對待

Treat others as you would like to be treated.

= Do unto others as you would have them do unto you.

（【諺】以希望別人對待你的方式來對待他人；己所不欲；勿施於人。）

19. (**D**) 依句意，選 (D) ***advice***〔ədˈvaɪs〕*n.* 忠告；建議。

而 (A) 機會，(B) 時間，

(C) result〔rɪˈzʌlt〕*n.* 結果，則不合句意。

20. (**B**) 依句意，選 (B) ***treated***「被對待」。

而 (A) notice〔ˈnotɪs〕*v.* 注意到，

(C) respect〔rɪˈspɛkt〕*v.* 尊敬，

(D) please〔pliz〕*v.* 取悅，則不合句意。

Test 16

Read the following passage and choose the best answer for each blank from the list below.

The concept of solitude（獨處）in the digital world is almost non-existent. In the world of digital technology, e-mail, social networking and online video games, information is meant to be ___1___. Solitude can be hard to recover ___2___ it has been given up. In this respect, new technologies have ___3___ our culture.

(　) 1. A. updated　B. received　C. shared　D. collected

(　) 2. A. though　B. until　C. once　D. before

(　) 3. A. respected　B. shaped　C. ignored　D. preserved

The desire to be connected has brought solitude as we've known it to a(n) ___4___. People have become so ___5___ in the world of networks and connections that people can often be contacted ___6___ they'd rather not be.

Today we can talk, text, e-mail, chat and blog（部落格）, not only from our ___7___, but from our mobile phones as well.

( ) 4. A. edge B. stage
C. end D. balance

( ) 5. A. sensitive B. intelligent
C. considerate D. reachable

( ) 6. A. even if B. only if
C. as if D. if only

( ) 7. A. media B. computers
C. databases D. monitors

People in most developed nations have become ___8___ on digital technology simply because they've grown accustomed to it, and at this point not ___9___ it would make them an outsiders. ___10___, many jobs and careers require people to be ___11___. From this point of view, technology has changed the culture of work. Being reachable might feel like a ___12___ to those who may not want to be able to be contacted at all times.

( ) 8. A. bent B. hard
C. keen D. dependent

( ) 9. A. finding B. using
C. protecting D. changing

( ) 10. A. Also B. Instead
C. Otherwise D. Somehow

( ) 11. A. connected B. trained
C. recommended D. interested

( ) 12. A. pleasure B. benefit
C. burden D. disappointment

I suppose the positive side is that solitude is still possible for anyone who __13__ wants it. Computers can be shut __14__ and mobile phones can be turned off. The ability to be "connected" and "on" has many __15__, as well as disadvantages. Travelers have ended up __16__ on mountains, and mobile phones have saved countless lives. They can also make people feel __17__ and forced to answer unwanted calls or __18__ to unwanted texts.

( ) 13. A. slightly B. hardly
C. merely D. really

( ) 14. A. out B. down
C. up D. in

( ) 15. A. aspects B. weaknesses
C. advantages D. exceptions

( ) 16. A. hidden B. lost
C. relaxed D. deserted

( ) 17. A. trapped B. excited
C. confused D. amused

( ) 18. A. turn B. submit
C. object D. reply

Attitudes towards our connectedness as a society ___19___ across generations. Some find today's technology a gift. Others consider it a curse. Regardless of anyone's view on the subject, it's hard to imagine what life would be like ___20___ daily advancements in technology.【2012 大陸江蘇卷】

( ) 19. A. vary B. arise
C. spread D. exist

( ) 20. A. beyond B. within
C. despite D. without

Test 16 詳解

(2012 大陸江蘇卷)

The concept *of solitude in the digital world* is *almost* non-existent.

在數位世界裡，獨處的概念是幾乎不存在的。

solitude ('sɑlə,tjud) *n.* 獨處；孤獨
digital ('dɪdʒɪtḷ) *adj.* 數位的
non-existent (nɑnɪg'zɪstənt) *adj.* 不存在的

In the world of digital technology, e-mail, social networking ***and*** *online video games,* information is meant to be shared.
1

在這個數位科技、電子郵件、社交網絡，還有線上遊戲的世界裡，資訊本來就是要被分享的。
1

digital technology 數位科技　***social networking*** 社交網絡
be meant to V. 目的是要…

1. (**C**) 依句意，選 (C) ***shared***「分享」。
而 (A) update (ʌp'det) *v.* 更新，(B) receive *v.* 收到，(D) collect *v.* 收集，均不合句意。

Solitude can be hard *to recover* ***once*** *it has been given up*.
2

一旦我們放棄了獨處，就很難再恢復了。
2

give up 放棄

2. (**C**) 依句意，選 (C) ***once***「一旦」。
而 (A) 雖然，(B) 直到，(D) 在～之前，皆不合句意。

In this respect, new technologies have shaped our culture.
3

從這方面來看，新科技已經塑造了我們的文化。
3

respect〔rɪ'spɛkt〕*n.* 方面　***in this respect*** 從這方面來看

3. (**B**) 依句意，選 (B) ***shaped***。
shape〔ʃep〕*v.* 塑造（= *form* = *build*）
而 (A) respect「尊敬」，(C) ignore〔ɪg'nor〕*v.* 忽視，
(D) preserve〔prɪ'zɜv〕*v.* 保存，則不合句意。

The desire *to be connected* has brought solitude ***as we've known it*** to an end
4

就如同我們所知道的，想要被聯繫上的渴望終結了獨處的可能。
4

desire〔dɪ'zaɪr〕*n.* 渴望　connect〔kə'nɛkt〕*v.* 連接；連結

4. (**C**) 依句意，選 (C) ***end***「結束」。

bring *sth.* ***to an end*** 結束某事；使某事變得不可能

而 (A) edge〔ɛdʒ〕*n.* 邊緣，(B) stage〔stedʒ〕*n.* 舞台，

(D) balance〔ˈbæləns〕*n.* 平衡，則不合句意。

People have become ***so*** reachable *in the world of networks* ***and*** *connections* ***that*** *people can often be contacted* ***even if*** *they'd rather not be.*

在這個網絡跟連結的世界裡，人們變得太隨手可及(5)，以致於即使(6)他們不希望如此，還是常常被聯絡上。

contact〔kɑnˈtækt〕*v.* 與…連結　　***would rather*** 寧願

so…that「如此…以致於」，that 引導副詞子句修飾前面副詞 so，而 so 是副詞，修飾形容詞 reachable。【詳見「文法寶典」p.516】

5. (**D**) 依句意，選 (D) ***reachable***「伸手可及的；可連絡到的」(= *accessible* = *attainable*)。

而 (A) sensitive〔ˈsɛnsətɪv〕*adj.* 敏感的，

(B) intelligent「聰明的」，

(C) considerate「體貼的」(= *thoughtful*)，則不合句意。

6. (**A**) 依句意，選 (A) ***even if***「即使」。

而 (B) only if「只有；除非」，(C) as if「就好像」，

(D) if only「但願」，則不合句意。

Today we can talk, text, e-mail, chat ***and*** blog, ***not only*** *from our* <u>*computers*</u>, ***but*** *from our mobile phones as well.*
7

現在我們不僅能用<u>電腦</u>，也能用手機說話、發簡訊、寄電子郵件、聊
7
天，還有寫部落格。

text〔tɛkst〕*v.* 傳簡訊　　e-mail〔ˈiˌmel〕*v.* 寄電子郵件

blog〔blɑg〕*n.* 部落格；網誌【在此當動詞，作「寫部落格」解】

not only…but (also) 是對等連接詞，表「不但…而且」，連接兩個文法作用相同的單字、片語或子句。在此是連接了兩個介系詞片語。【詳見「文法寶典」p.467】

7.（**B**）依句意，選(B) ***computers***「電腦」。

而 (A) media〔ˈmidɪə〕*n. pl.* 媒體，

(C) database〔ˈdetəˌbes〕*n.* 資料庫，

(D) monitor〔ˈmɑnətɚ〕*n.* 顯示器；螢幕，則不合句意。

People in most developed nations have become <u>dependent</u>
8
on digital technology *simply* ***because*** *they've grown accustomed to it*, ***and*** *at this point* not <u>using</u> it would make them an outsiders.
9

大部分已開發國家的人都變得很<u>依賴</u>數位科技，只是因爲他們已經
8
逐漸習慣，而在此時不<u>使用</u>數位科技的話，只會讓他們變成局外人。
9

developed nations 已開發國家　　grow (gro) *v.* 變得
grow accustomed to 變得習慣於…　　***at this point*** 在此時
outsider ('aʊt,saɪdɚ) *n.* 局外人

8. (**D**) 依句意，選 (D) ***dependent*** (dɪ'pɛndənt) *adj.* 依賴的。
而 (A) bent (bɛnt) *adj.* 彎曲的；專心的，
(B) hard (hɑrd) *adj.* 困難的，
(C) keen (kin) *adj.* 熱衷的；渴望的，則不合句意。

9. (**B**) 依句意，選 (B) ***using***「使用」。(C) protecting「保護」。

Also (10), many jobs ***and*** careers require people to be connected (11).
而且 (10)，許多工作和職業都要求要能被聯繫 (11) 上。

10. (**A**) 依句意，選 (A) ***Also***「而且」。
而 (B) Instead「取而代之；反而」，(C) Otherwise「否則」，
(D) Somehow「不知道爲什麼」，則不合句意。

11. (**A**) 依句意，選 (A) ***connected***「被聯繫上的」。
(C) recommend (,rɛkə'mɛnd) *v.* 推薦。

From this point of view, technology has changed the culture *of work*. Being reachable might feel like a burden (12) to those ***who*** *may not want to be able to be contacted at all times.*

從這個觀點來看，科技已經改變了工作的文化。隨時能被連絡上的這件事，對那些不想要隨時都被聯繫到的人而言，可能會覺得像是一個負擔。
12

from this point of view 從這個觀點來看
contact〔ˈkɑntækt〕*v.* 連絡

12.（**C**）依句意，選 (C) ***burden***〔ˈbɝdn̩〕*n.* 負擔。
而 (A) pleasure「樂趣」，(B) benefit〔ˈbɛnəfɪt〕*n.* 利益，(D) disappointment「失望」，則不合句意。

I suppose *the positive side is* ***that*** *solitude is still possible for anyone* ***who*** *really wants it.*
13

我想好的一面就是，獨處對於那些真正想要它的人，依然是有可能的。
13

suppose〔səˈpoz〕*v.* 猜想　　positive〔ˈpɑzətɪv〕*adj.* 正面的
positive side 好的一面

13.（**D**）依句意，選 (D) ***really***「真正地」（= *truly* = *indeed*）。
而 (A) slightly〔ˈslaɪtlɪ〕*adv.* 稍微地，
(B) hardly「幾乎不」（= *seldom* = *barely* = *rarely*），
(C) merely「僅僅；只是」（= *only* = *simply*），則不合句意。

Computers can be shut down ***and*** mobile phones can be turned off.
14

電腦可以關機，而且手機也可以關機。
14

turn off 關掉（電源）

14. (**B**) 依句意，選 (B) ***shut down***「關掉（機器）」。
而 (A) shut out「關在外面」，(C) shut up「閉嘴」，
(D) shut in「關在裡面」，則不合句意。
shut〔ʃʌt〕*v.* 關；閉【三態變化爲：shut-shut-shut】

The ability *to be* "*connected*" *and* "*on*" has many advantages,
15
as well as disadvantages.

能夠被聯繫上，有很多的優點跟缺點。
15

as well as「以及」是對等連接詞，連接兩個文法作用相同的單字、片語或子句。【詳見「文法寶典」p.467】

15. (**C**) 依句意，選 (C) ***advantages***「優點」。
而 (A) aspect〔ˈæspɛkt〕*n.* 方面，
(B) weakness〔ˈwiknɪs〕*n.* 弱點，
(D) exception「例外」，則不合句意。。

Travelers have ended up lost *on mountains*, ***and*** mobile
16
phones have saved countless lives.

旅人可能會在山中迷路，而手機已經拯救了無數的生命。
16

end up 最後（變成）；以…結果

16.（**B**）依句意，選 (B) ***lost***「迷路的」。
而 (A) hidden「被隱藏的」，(C) relaxed「感到放鬆的」，
(D) deserted「被拋棄的；荒蕪的」（= *uninhabited*
= *desolate* = *barren*），則不合句意。

They can *also* make people feel <u>trapped</u> (17) ***and*** forced to answer unwanted calls ***or*** <u>reply</u> (18) to unwanted texts.

它們也讓人感覺<u>受到限制</u>(17)，而且還要被迫去接不想接的電話，或<u>回覆</u>(18)不想要的簡訊。

force〔fors〕*v.* 強迫　　answer〔ˈænsɚ〕*v.* 接（電話）
unwanted〔ʌnˈwɑntɪd〕*adj.* 不想要的　　text〔tɛkst〕*n.* 簡訊

17.（**A**）依句意，選 (A) ***trapped***「被限制住的」。
trap〔træp〕*v.* 使困住
而 (B) excited「感到興奮的」，
(C) confused「感到困惑的」（= *baffled* = *perplexed*
= *puzzled*），
(D) amused「感到愉快的」，則不合句意。。

18.（**D**）依句意，選 (D) ***reply to***「回覆」。
而 (A) turn to「向～求助」，(B) submit to「向～屈服」，
(C) object to「反對」，則不合句意。

Attitudes *towards our connectedness as a society* vary (19) *across generations.*

人們對於整個社會都被連結起來的看法，每個世代都不同(19)。

attitude〔'ætə,tjud〕*n.* 態度；看法
towards〔tordz〕*prep.* 對於
connectedness〔kə'nɛktɪdnɪs〕*n.* 有關連；能接通

19.（**A**）依句意，選 (A) ***vary***「不同」。
vary across generations 每個世代不同
（= *vary from generation to generation*
= *differ from generation to generation*）
而 (B) arise〔ə'raɪz〕*v.* 發生，
(C) spread〔sprɛd〕*v.* 散播，
(D) exist〔ɪg'zɪst〕*v.* 存在，則不合句意。

Some find today's technology a gift. Others consider it a curse.

有些人認爲現今的科技是個禮物，有些人認爲它是一個詛咒。

find A B 認爲 A 是 B
consider A (to be) B 認爲 A 是 B
curse〔kɝs〕*n.* 詛咒

Regardless of anyone's view on the subject, it's hard to imagine ***what*** *life would be like* without *daily advancements in technology*.
20

不論大家對於這個議題的看法是什麼，我們都很難想像，科技如果沒有每天進步，我們的生活將會變成什麼樣子。
20

regardless of 不管；不論（= *in spite of* = *despite* = *notwithstanding*） view〔vju〕*n.* 看法
on〔ɑn〕*prep.* 關於（= *about* = *regarding* = *concerning* = *respecting* = *touching on*）
subject〔ˈsʌbdʒɪkt〕*n.* 主題；議題（= *topic* = *issue*）
imagine〔ɪˈmædʒɪn〕*v.* 想像
daily〔ˈdelɪ〕*adj.* 每天的（= *everyday*）
advancement〔ədˈvænsmənt〕*n.* 進步（= *improvement* = *progress*）

20.（**D**）依句意，選(D) ***without***「如果沒有」。
而(A) beyond「在…之外」，
(B) within「在…之內」，
(C) despite「儘管」，則不合句意。

Test 17

Read the following passage and choose the best answer for each blank from the list below.

I often read of incidents of misunderstanding or conflict. I'm left __1__. Why do these people create mistrust and problems, especially with those from other __2__?

( ) 1. A. interested B. pleased
C. puzzled D. excited

( ) 2. A. parties B. cities
C. villages D. races

I grew up in Kuala Lumpur in the early 1960s, __3__ children from different races and religions played and studied __4__ in harmony. At that time my family lived a stone's __5__ from Ismail's. And no one was bothered that Ismail was a Malay Muslim and I was an Indian Hindu—we just __6__ our differences. Perhaps, our elders had not filled our heads with unnecessary advice, well __7__ or otherwise.

( ) 3. A. why B. which
C. how D. when

( ) 4. A. together B. around
C. alone D. apart

( ) 5. A. drop B. throw
C. move D. roll

( ) 6. A. refused B. made
C. sought D. accepted

( ) 7. A. paid B. meant
C. preserved D. treated

We were nine when we became friends. During the school holidays, we'd __8__ the countryside on our bicycles, hoping to __9__ the unexpected. At times Ismail would accompany my family as we made a rare shopping trip to town. We were glad to have his __10__.

( ) 8. A. explore B. search
C. discover D. desert

( ) 9. A. get through B. deal with
C. come across D. take away

( ) 10. A. arrival B. choice
C. effort D. company

When I was twelve, my family moved to Johor. Ismail's family later returned to their village, and I ___11___ touch with him.

( ) 11. A. lost B. gained
C. developed D. missed

One spring afternoon in 1983, I stopped a taxi in Kuala Lumpur. I ___12___ my destination. The driver acknowledged my ___13___ but did not move off. Instead, he looked ___14___ at me. "Raddar?" he said, using my childhood nickname（綽號）. I was astonished at being so ___15___ addressed（稱呼）. It was Ismail! Even after two ___16___ we still recognized each other. Grasping his shoulder, I felt a true affection, something ___17___ to describe.

( ) 12. A. stated B. ordered
C. decided D. chose

( ) 13. A. attempts B. instructions
C. opinions D. arrangements

( ) 14. A. anxiously B. carelessly
C. disappointedly D. fixedly

( ) 15. A. familiarly B. strangely
C. fully D. coldly

( ) 16. A. departures B. months
C. years D. decades

( ) 17. A. possible B. funny
C. hard D. clear

If we can allow our children to be __18__ without prejudice, they'll build friendships with people, regardless of race or religion, who will be __19__ their side through thick and thin. On such friendships are societies built, and __20__ we can truly be, as William Shakespeare once wrote, "we happy few, we band of brothers."【2012 大陸福建卷】

( ) 18. A. them B. themselves
C. us D. ourselves

( ) 19. A. from B. by
C. with D. against

( ) 20. A. still B. otherwise
C. then D. instead

Test 17 詳解

(2012 大陸福建卷)

I *often* read of incidents *of misunderstanding* ***or*** *conflict*. I'm left puzzled.
1

我經常看到誤會或衝突引起的事件。我總是很困惑。
1

incident〔ˈɪnsədənt〕*n.* 事件
misunderstanding〔ˌmɪsʌndɚˈstændɪŋ〕*n.* 誤會
conflict〔ˈkɑnflɪkt〕*n.* 衝突；紛爭
leave〔liv〕*v.* 使處於（某種狀態）
sb. ***be left***… 某人呈現…的狀態

1.（**C**）依句意，選 (C) ***puzzled***「感到困惑的」（= *baffled* = *confused* = *perplexed* = *bewildered*）。
(B) pleased〔plizd〕*adj.* 感到滿意的

Why do these people create mistrust ***and*** problems, *especially with those from other races*?
2

爲何這些人要引起不信任跟問題，尤其是跟那些其他種族的人?
2

especially〔əˈspɛʃəlɪ〕*adv.* 尤其是
mistrust〔mɪsˈtrʌst〕*n.* 不信任

2.（**D**）依句意，選(D) ***races***〔ˈresɪz〕*n.pl.* 種族。

(A) party〔ˈpɑrtɪ〕*n.* 政黨，(C) village〔ˈvɪlɪdʒ〕*n.* 村莊。

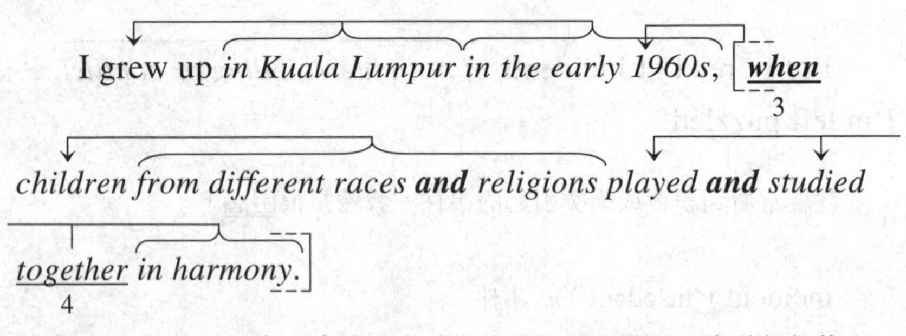

我在 1960 年代早期在吉隆坡長大，當時不同種族跟不同宗教信仰的小孩，都很合諧地一起遊戲跟念書。

Kuala Lumpur〔ˌkwɑlə ˈlʊmpʊr〕*n.* 吉隆坡【馬來西亞的首都】

religion〔rɪˈlɪdʒɪən〕*n.* 宗教　　***in harmony*** 合諧地

3.（**D**）依句意，選(D)。

表「時間」的關係副詞 when 引導先行詞為 the early 1960s 的形容詞子句。【詳見「文法寶典」p.242】

4.（**A**）依句意，選(A) ***together***「一起」。

而 (B) around *adv.* 在附近，(C) alone〔əˈlon〕*adv.* 獨自，(D) apart〔əˈpɑrt〕*adv.* 分開地，則不合句意。

At that time my family lived *a stone's throw from Ismail's*.
5

那時候我們家距離伊斯梅爾家只有咫尺之遠。
5

Ismail's = Ismail's family

5. (**B**) 依句意，選 (B) ***throw***。

a stone's throw 字面的意思是「投石能到達的距離」，像中文說的「一投石的距離」，也就是「近距離；咫尺之遠」。

而 (A) drop〔drɑp〕*n.* 掉落，(C) move〔muv〕*n.* 移動，(D) roll〔rol〕*n.* 滾動，則不合句意。

And no one was bothered ***that*** *Ismail was a Malay Muslim* ***and*** *I was an Indian Hindu*—we *just* accepted (6) our differences.

而且沒有人對於伊斯梅爾是馬來籍回教徒，而我是印度籍印度教徒而感到困擾——我們接受 (6) 了彼此的差異。

bother〔ˈbɑðɚ〕*v.* 使困擾　Malay〔məˈle〕*adj.* 馬來人的

Muslim〔ˈmʌzlɪm〕*n.* 回教徒　***Malay Muslim*** 馬來籍回教徒

Indian〔ˈɪndɪən〕*adj.* 印度的　Hindu〔ˈhɪndu〕*n.* 印度教徒

Indian Hindu 印度籍印度教徒

6. (**D**) 依句意，選 (D) ***accepted***「接受」。而 (A) 拒絕，

(C) sought〔sɔt〕是 seek「尋求」的過去式，則不合句意。

Perhaps, our elders had not filled our heads *with unnecessary advice*, *well meant (7) or otherwise.*

或許我們的長輩並沒有灌輸我們不必要的建議，無論是出於好意或是惡意。
7

elder〔ˈɛldɚ〕*n.* 年長者　*one's* ***elders*** 前輩；長輩
fill〔fɪl〕*v.* 使充滿；填滿
advice〔ədˈvaɪs〕*n.* 忠告；建議
or otherwise 或相反

7.（**B**）依句意，選 (B) ***meant***「意味；立意」。
well meant 出於好意的（= *well-meant*）
而 (A) well paid「薪水高的」，
(C) preserve〔prɪˈzɝv〕*v.* 保存，
(D) treat〔trit〕*v.* 對待，則不合句意。

We were nine ***when*** *we became friends. During the school holidays*, we'd explored the countryside *on our bicycles*,
8
hoping to come across the unexpected.
9

我們九歲的時候就成爲朋友了。在學校放假時，我們會騎腳踏車去鄉下探索，希望能巧遇我們沒預期會出現的事物。
8　9

…, *hoping to come across*…. 源自…, ***and we*** *hoped to come across*….。
對等子句主詞相同時，分詞構句可代替合句中另一對等子句，保留一主詞即可。【詳見「文法寶典」p.459】

8. (**A**) 依句意，選 (A) ***explore*** ﹝ɪk'splor﹞*v.* 探索。
而 (B) search ﹝sɝtʃ﹞*v.* 尋找，
(C) discover ﹝dɪ'skʌvɚ﹞*v.* 發現，
(D) desert ﹝dɪ'zɝt﹞*v.* 拋棄，則不合句意。

9. (**C**) 依句意，選 (C) ***come across***「偶然遇到」(= *bump into* = *run into* = *encounter*)。
而 (A) get through「通過」，(B) deal with「應付；處理」，(D) take away「拿走」，皆不合句意。

At times Ismail would accompany my family ***as*** *we made a rare shopping trip to town.* We were glad to have his company. (10)

當我們偶爾去城鎮逛街的時候，有時候伊斯梅爾會陪伴我的家人。我們都很樂於他的陪伴。(10)

at times 有時候 (= *from time to time* = *somtimes* = *now and again* = *occasionally* = *once in a while*)
accompany ﹝ə'kʌmpənɪ﹞*v.* 陪伴
make a shopping trip 逛街

10. (**D**) 依句意，選 (D) ***company*** ﹝'kʌmpənɪ﹞主要意思是「公司」，在這裡作「陪伴」解。
而 (A) arrival ﹝ə'raɪvḷ﹞*n.* 到達，(B) choice *n.* 選擇，
(C) effort ﹝'ɛfɚt﹞*n.* 努力，則不合句意。

When I was twelve, my family moved to Johor. Ismail's family *later* returned to their village, ***and*** I lost touch *with him*.
11

當我十二歲的時候，我們家就搬到了柔佛。伊斯梅爾他們家之後也回到他們的村莊，然後我就跟他失去聯繫了。
11

move〔 muv 〕*v.* 搬家　Johor〔 dʒə'hɔr 〕*n.* 柔佛【馬來西亞地名】

11.（**A**）依句意，選 (A) ***lost***「失去」。
***lost contact with** sb.* 和某人失去連絡
(C) developed「發展」。

One spring afternoon in 1983, I stopped a taxi *in Kuala Lumpur*. I stated my destination.
12

在 1983 年春天的一個下午，我在吉隆坡攔了一台計程車。我說了我的目的地。
12

stop〔 stɑp 〕*v.* 使停下　destination〔ˌdɛstə'neʃən 〕*n.* 目的地

12.（**A**）依句意，選 (A) ***stated***「說」。

The driver acknowledged my instructions ***but*** did not move off. *Instead*, he looked *fixedly* at me.
13 14

司機確認了我的指示卻沒有移動。他反而眼珠子動也不動地盯著我看。
13 14

acknowledge〔əkˈnɑlɪdʒ〕*v.* 確認；認可　　***move off*** 移動
instead〔ɪnˈstɛd〕*adv.* 反而；代替的是（= *rather*）

13.（**B**）依句意，選 (B) ***instructions***〔ɪnˈstrʌkʃənz〕*n. pl.* 指示。
而 (A) attempt〔əˈtɛmp〕*n.* 嘗試，(C) opinion *n.* 意見，
(D) arrangement〔əˈrendʒmənt〕*n.* 安排，則不合句意。

14.（**D**）依句意，選 (D) ***fixedly***〔ˈfɪkstlɪ〕*adv.* 動也不動地。
而 (A) anxiously〔ˈæŋkʃəslɪ〕*adv.* 焦慮地；熱切地，
(B) 不小心地，(C) disappointedly *adv.* 感到失望地，
均不合句意。

"Raddar?" he said, *using my childhood nickname*. I was astonished at being *so* familiarly (15) addressed. It was Ismail!

「拉達？」他說，用我小時候的綽號。我很驚訝於被如此親密地 (15) 稱呼著。是伊斯梅爾！

…, *using my childhood nickname* 源自…, ***and he*** *used my childhood nickname*。對等子句主詞相同時，分詞構句可代替合句中另一對等子句，保留一主詞即可。【詳見「文法寶典」p.459】

nickname〔ˈnɪkˌnem〕*v.* 綽號
astonished〔əˈstɑnɪʃt〕*adj.* 驚訝的（= *astounded* = *amazed* = *surprised* = *stunned* = *overwhelmed* = *startled*）
address〔əˈdrɛs〕*v.* 稱呼

15. (**A**) 依句意，選 (A) ***familiarly*** [fə'mɪljəlɪ] *adv.* 親密地。

Even after two *decades* we *still* recognized each other.
16

即使在二十年後，我們依然認得出彼此。
16

16. (**D**) 依句意，選 (D) ***decades***。decade ['dɛked] *n.* 十年
因為前面作者說自己生長於 1960 年代，事件發生時間點是 1983 年，總計約二十幾年。
(A) departure [dɪ'pɑrtʃɚ] *n.* 出發

Grasping his shoulder, I felt a true affection, *something* *hard* *to describe*.
17

當我抓著他肩膀時，我感覺到一份真誠的感情，一種難以形容的感覺。
17

grasp [græsp] *v.* 抓住　　affection [ə'fɛkʃən] *n.* 情感

Grasping his shoulder 源自 ***When I*** *grasped his shoulder*，前後主詞相同時，副詞子句可改為分詞構句。

【詳見「文法寶典」p.458】

17. (**C**) 依句意，選 (C) ***hard*** [hɑrd] *adj.* 困難的。
而 (A) 可能的，(B) 好笑的，(D) 清楚的，則不合句意。

***If** we can allow our children to be themselves without*
18

prejudice, they'll build friendships *with people*, *regardless of race or religion*, ***who** will be by their side through thick and thin.*
19

如果我們能讓我們的孩子沒有偏見地做自己，他們將會與人們建立友誼，不論種族或宗教信仰，而那些人將會在他們身旁與他們同甘共苦過人生的起伏。
(18: 自己; 19: 旁)

allow (əˈlaʊ) *v.* 讓　　prejudice (ˈprɛdʒədɪs) *n.* 偏見
regardless of 無論　　***through thick and thin*** 同甘共苦

18. (**B**) 依句意，選(B) ***themselves***「他們自己」。

19. (**B**) 依句意，選(B) ***by***。***by** one's **side*** 在某人身邊

On such friendships are societies built, ***and** then* we can *truly* be, *as William Shakespeare once wrote*, "we happy few, we band of brothers."
20

社會建立在如此的友誼之上，然後我們就能夠眞的如同莎士比亞寫的那樣:「我們是少數幾位很快樂的人，我們是一群兄弟。」
(20: 然後)

***build** sth.* ***on** sth.* 把某事物建立在某事物之上

【例】Our relationship is *built on* trust.

（我們的關係建立在互相信任的基礎上。）

William Shakespeare 莎士比亞【知名劇作家】

band〔bænd〕*n.* 一群；一夥

On such friendships are societies built 是 *Societies are built on such friendships* 的倒裝句。【詳見「文法寶典」p.631】

We happy few, we band of brothers. 意指 *We are happy few, we are a band of brothers.*【出自莎士比亞劇本「亨利五世」(Henry V)】

原文參照如下：

From this day to the ending of the world,
從今天直到世界末日，
But we in it shall be remembered.
我們將永遠會被記住。
We few, we happy few, we band of brothers.
我們，我們快樂的少數人，我們是一群兄弟。
For he today that sheds his blood with me
凡是與我一同浴血奮戰過的
shall be my brother.
就是我生死與共的手足。

20.（**C**）依句意，選 (C) ***then***「然後」。
而 (A) 仍然，(B) otherwise〔ˈʌðɚˌwaɪz〕*adv.* 否則，(D) instead *adv.* 取而代之；反而，皆不合句意。

Test 18

Read the following passage and choose the best answer for each blank from the list below.

If you want to learn a new language, the very first thing to think about is why. Do you need it for a ___1___ reason, such as your job or your studies? ___2___ perhaps you're interested in the ___3___, films or music of a different country and you know how much it will help to have a ___4___ of the language.

( ) 1. A. technical B. political C. practical D. physical

( ) 2. A. After B. So C. Though D. Or

( ) 3. A. literature B. transport C. agriculture D. medicine

( ) 4. A. view B. knowledge C. form D. database

Most people learn best using a variety of ___5___, but traditional classes are an ideal（理想的）start for many people. They ___6___ an environment where you can practice under the ___7___ of someone who's good at the language. We all lead ___8___ lives and learning a language takes ___9___. You will have more success if you study regularly, so try to develop a ___10___. It doesn't matter if you haven't got long. Becoming fluent in a language will take years, but learning to get by takes ___11___.

( ) 5. A. paintings B. regulations
C. methods D. computers

( ) 6. A. protect B. change
C. respect D. provide

( ) 7. A. control B. command
C. guidance D. pressure

( ) 8. A. busy B. happy
C. simple D. normal

( ) 9. A. courage B. time
C. energy D. place

( ) 10. A. theory B. business
C. routine D. project

( ) 11. A. some risks B. a lot less
C. some notes D. a lot more

Many people start learning a language and soon give up. "I'm too __12__," they say. Yes, children do learn languages more __13__ than adults, but research has shown that you can learn a language at any __14__. And learning is good for the health of your brain, too. I've also heard people __15__ about the mistakes they make when __16__. Well, relax and laugh about your mistakes, __17__ you're much less likely to make them again.

( ) 12. A. old B. nervous
C. weak D. tired

( ) 13. A. closely B. quickly
C. privately D. quietly

( ) 14. A. age B. speed
C. distance D. school

( ) 15. A. worry B. hesitate
C. think D. quarrel

( ) 16. A. singing B. working
C. bargaining D. learning

( ) 17. A. if B. and
C. but D. before

Learning a new language is never ___18___. But with some work and devotion, you'll make progress. And you'll be ___19___ by the positive reaction of some people when you say just a few words in ___20___ language. Good luck!【2013 大陸安徽卷】

( ) 18. A. tiresome B. hard
C. interesting D. easy

( ) 19. A. blamed B. amazed
C. interrupted D. informed

( ) 20. A. their B. his
C. our D. your

Test 18 詳解

(2013 年大陸安徽卷)

If you want to learn a new language, the *very* first thing *to think about* is why.

如果你想要學一個新的語言，第一件要思考的事就是爲什麼。

If 引導副詞子句，修飾完全不及物動詞 is。
very 常用的意思是「非常」，在這裡作「眞正地；正是」解，強調 first，如：It is the ***very*** last thing I expected.（那完全是出乎我意料之外的事。）

Do you need it *for a practical reason, such as your job* ***or*** *your studies*?
1

你需要它是因爲一個實際的原因，像是你的工作或是學業嗎？
1

for…reason 表示「因爲…的理由」，如：for no reason「無緣無故」。
studies〔ˈstʌdɪz〕*n. pl.* 功課；學業

1.（**C**）依句意，選 (C) ***practical***〔ˈpræktɪkl̩〕*adj.* 實際的。
而 (A) technical〔ˈtɛknɪkl̩〕*adj.* 技術的，

(B) political〔pə'lɪtɪkḷ〕*adj.* 政治的，

(D) physical〔'fɪzɪkḷ〕*adj.* 身體的，則不合句意。

Or *perhaps* you're interested in the literature, films ***or*** music *of a different country* ***and*** you know ***how much*** *it will help to have a* knowledge *of the language*.

或是你可能對一個不同國家的文學、電影，或是音樂感興趣，而且你知道了解該語言會有多少的幫助。

it will help to V. 表示「…會有幫助」，it 爲虛主詞，代替後面的 to V.。

2. (**D**) 依句意，選 (D) ***Or***「或者；或是」。

3. (**A**) 依句意，選 (A) ***literature***〔'lɪtərətʃə〕*n.* 文學。

而 (B) transport〔'trænsport〕*n.* 運輸，

(C) agriculture〔'ægrɪˌkʌltʃə〕*n.* 農業，

(D) medicine〔'mɛdəsṇ〕*n.* 醫學，則不合句意。

4. (**B**) 依句意，選 (B) ***knowledge***「知識；了解」。

have a knowledge of 熟知；了解

一般來説，knowledge 爲「不可數名詞」，但用於某方面的知識或了解時，則可以加上冠詞 a(n)，如：

You need to have ***a basic knowledge of*** computers.

（你需要有電腦的基本知識。）

Most people learn *best using a variety of methods*, ***but***
5

traditional classes are an ideal start *for many people*.

大多數的人用各種不同的方法學習效果最好，但是傳統的課程對
5
很多人來說是個理想的開始。

a variety of 各種的；各式各樣的

traditional〔trəˈdɪʃənl̩〕*adj.* 傳統的

ideal〔aɪˈdiəl〕*adj.* 理想的

5.（ **C** ）依句意，選 (C) ***methods***〔ˈmɛθədz〕*n. pl.* 方法。
而 (A) 畫，(B) regulation〔ˌrɛgjəˈleʃən〕*n.* 規定，
(D) 電腦，則不合句意。

They provide an environment [***where*** *you can practice under*
6

the guidance of someone ***who****'s good at the language.*]
7

它們提供了一個環境，讓你可以在擅長該語言的人的指導之下練習。
6 7

where 爲關係副詞，引導形容詞子句，修飾 environment，
也可以用 in which 代替。

6. (**D**) 依句意，選 (D) ***provide***「提供」。

   而 (A) 保護，(B) 改變，(C) 尊敬，則不合句意。

7. (**C**) 依句意，選 (C) ***guidance***〔ˈgaɪdəns〕*n.* 指導。

   under the guidance of 在…的指導下

   而 (A) 控制，(B) command〔kəˈmænd〕*n.* 命令；指揮，

   (D) pressure〔ˈprɛʃɚ〕*n.* 壓力，則不合句意。

We all lead busy (8) lives ***and*** learning a language takes time (9).

我們都過著忙碌的 (8) 生活，而且學語言需要時間 (9)。

lead a~life 過~的生活　take〔tek〕*v.* 需要；花費

8. (**A**) 依句意，選 (A) ***busy***「忙碌的」。

   (D) normal〔ˈnɔrml̩〕*adj.* 正常的

9. (**B**) 依句意，選 (B) ***time***「時間」。

   而 (A) courage〔ˈkɝɪdʒ〕*n.* 勇氣，

   (C) energy〔ˈɛnɚdʒɪ〕*n.* 活力；精力，

   (D) take place「發生」，則不合句意。

You will have more success ***if you study regularly***, ***so*** try to develop a routine (10).

如果你有規律地研讀，你會更成功，所以要試著養成習慣 (10)。

regularly〔'rɛgjələlɪ〕*adv.* 定期地
develop〔dɪ'vɛləp〕*v.* 培養

10.(**C**) 依句意，選(C) ***routine***〔ru'tin〕*n.* 例行公事；常規；慣例。
而(A) theory〔'θiərɪ〕*n.* 理論，(B) 生意，
(D) project〔'prɑdʒɛkt〕*n.* 計畫，則不合句意。

It doesn't matter ***if*** *you haven't got long*. Becoming fluent in a language will take years, ***but*** learning to get by takes *a lot* less. (11)

沒有很長的時間也沒關係。語言要講得流利需要好幾年，但是要學到能夠勉強應付所需要的，所花的時間就少很多。(11)

It 爲虛主詞，代替 if 所引導的名詞子句 if you haven't got long。
have got 有　　long〔lɔŋ〕*n.* 長時間
fluent〔'fluənt〕*adj.* 流利的　　***get by*** 勉強應付

11.(**B**) 依句意，選(B) ***a lot less***「少很多」。
a lot 修飾比較級 less。可以修飾比較級的副詞還有：(very) much, yet, (by) far, still, a great deal, far and away, even, a little 等。【詳見「文法寶典」p.207】
而(A) risk〔rɪsk〕*n.* 風險，(C) note〔not〕*n.* 筆記，
(D) a lot more「更多」，則不合句意。

Many people start learning a language ***and soon*** give up.

"I'm *too* old," they say.
12

很多人開始學語言，然後很快就放棄了。「我太老了，」他們說。
12

12. (**A**) 依句意，選 (A) ***old*** *adj.* 年老的。

而 (B) nervous〔ˈnɝvəs〕*adj.* 緊張的，

(C) weak〔wik〕*adj.* 虛弱的，

(D) tired *adj.* 疲倦的，則不合句意。

Yes, children do learn languages *more quickly* ***than*** *adults*, ***but***
13

research has shown ***that*** *you can learn a language at any age.*
14

沒錯，孩童的確學語言比成人還快，但是研究顯示，你可以在任何年齡學習語言。
13 14

do + V. 的 do 用於加強語氣，表示「的確；眞的」。

13. (**B**) 依句意，選 (B) ***quickly***「快速地」。

而 (A) closely〔ˈkloslɪ〕*adv.* 密切地，

(C) privately〔ˈpraɪvɪtlɪ〕*adv.* 私下地，

(D) quietly〔ˈkwaɪətlɪ〕*adv.* 安靜地，則不合句意。

14. (**A**) 依句意，選 (A) ***age***「年齡」。

(B) speed〔spid〕*n.* 速度，(C) distance〔ˈdɪstəns〕*n.* 距離

And learning is good *for the health of your brain, too*. I've *also* heard people <u>worry</u> about the mistakes *they make* ***when*** <u>*learning*</u>.
15 16

而且學語言也有助於你腦部的健康。我也聽過有人<u>擔心</u>他們在<u>學</u>語言時所犯的錯誤。
15 16

hear + sb. + V. 表示「聽到某人～」。感官動詞之後，用原形動詞做受詞補語，常見的感官動詞還有：see, feel, watch, behold（看）, perceive（察覺）, observe（觀察）, notice（注意到）, overhear（偷聽到）等。【詳見「文法寶典」p.420】
when learning 是由 when *they are* learning 省略而來。

15.（**A**）依句意，選 (A) ***worry***。***worry about*** 擔心
而 (B) hesitate〔ˈhɛzəˌtet〕*v.* 猶豫，
(C) think about「考慮」，(D) quarrel〔ˈkwɔrəl〕*n.* 爭吵，
則不合句意。

16.（**D**）依句意，選 (D) ***learning***「學習」。

Well, relax and laugh *about your mistakes*, <u>***and***</u> you're *much less* likely to make them.
17

嗯，放輕鬆，笑一笑你犯的錯，你<u>就</u>比較不可能再犯一樣的錯。
17

laugh about 對…感到好笑而發笑　***be likely to V.*** 可能～

17. (**B**) 本題考的是「祈使句表條件」的句型：

祈使句, and + S. + V.
= If + S. + V., …

也可寫成：Well, if you relax and laugh about your mistakes, you're less likely to make them.

Learning a new language is *never* easy (18). ***But*** *with some work* ***and*** *devotion*, you'll make progress.

學習一個新的語言絕不是件容易的(18)事。但是如果你肯努力和投入，你就將會進步。

work (wɜk) *n.* 努力

make progress 進步 (= *improve* = *make improvement*)

18. (**D**) 依句意，選 (D) ***easy***「容易的」。

(A) tiresome (ˈtaɪrsəm) *adj.* 令人厭煩的；易使人疲倦的

And you'll be amazed (19) *by the positive reaction of some people* ***when*** *you say just a few words in* their (20) *language*. Good luck!

而當你用他們的語言說出一些話時，你將會對於一些人正面的反應感到
20
驚訝。祝你好運！
19

positive〔ˈpɑzətɪv〕*adj.* 正面的（= *good* = *favorable*〔ˈfevərəbḷ〕= *encouraging* = *constructive*〔kənˈstrʌktɪv〕)

reaction〔rɪˈækʃən〕*n.* 反應

re (*back*) + action（動作）= reaction（= *response* = *reply* = *feedback*）

just〔dʒʌst〕*adv.* 只（= *only* = *merely* = *simply*）

in〔ɪn〕*prep.* 用（語言）

Good luck! 祝你好運！

19.（**B**）依句意，選 (B) ***amazed***。amaze〔əˈmez〕*v.* 使驚訝
a + maze（迷宮）= amaze，迷宮「使」人「驚訝」。
（= *surprise* = *shock* = *astonish*〔əˈstɑnɪʃ〕= *astound*〔əˈstaʊnd〕= *stun* = *startle*）
而 (A) blame〔blem〕*v.* 責備，
(C) interrupt〔ˌɪntəˈrʌpt〕*v.* 打斷，
(D) inform〔ɪnˈfɔrm〕*v.* 通知，則不合句意。

20.（**A**）依句意，選 (A) ***their***「他們的」。

Test 19

Read the following passage and choose the best answer for each blank from the list below.

Research has shown that two-thirds of human conversation is taken up not with discussion of the cultural or political problems of the day, not heated debates about films we've just watched or books we've just finished reading, but plain and simple __1__.

( ) 1. A. claim B. description
C. gossip D. language

Language is our greatest treasure as a species, and what do we __2__ do with it? We gossip. About others' behaviour and private lives, such as who's doing what with whom, who's in and who's out—and why; how to deal with difficult __3__ situations involving children, lovers, and colleagues.

( ) 2. A. occasionally B. habitually
C. independently D. originally

( ) 3. A. social B. political
C. historical D. cultural

So why are we keen on gossiping? Are we just natural ___4___, of both time and words? Or do we talk a lot about nothing in particular simply to avoid facing up to the really important issues of life? That's not the case according to Professor Robin Dunbar. In fact, in his latest book, *Grooming, Gossip and the Evolution of Language*, the psychologist says gossip is one of these really ___5___ issues.

( ) 4. A. admirers B. masters
C. users D. wasters

( ) 5. A. vital B. sensitive
C. ideal D. difficult

Dunbar ___6___ the traditional view that language was developed by men at an early stage of social development in order to organize their manly hunting activities more effectively, or even to promote the exchange of poetic stories about their origins and the supernatural. Instead he suggests that language evolved among women. We don't spend two-thirds of our time gossiping just because we can talk, argues Dunbar— ___7___, he goes on to say, language evolved specifically to allow us to gossip.

( ) 6. A. confirms B. rejects
C. outlines D. broadens

( ) 7. A. for instance B. in addition
C. on the contrary D. as a result

Dunbar arrived at his cheery theory by studying the ___8___ of higher primates（靈長類動物）, such as monkeys. By means of grooming—cleaning the fur by brushing it, monkeys form groups with other individuals on whom they can rely for support in the event of some kind of conflict within the group or ___9___ from outside it.

( ) 8. A. motivation B. appearance
C. emotion D. behaviour

( ) 9. A. attack B. contact
C. inspection D. assistance

As we human beings evolved from a particular branch of the primate family, Dunbar ___10___ that at one time in our history we did much the same. Grouping together made sense because the bigger the group, the greater the ___11___ it provided; on the other hand, the bigger the group, the greater the stresses of living close to others. Grooming helped to ___12___ the pressure and calm everybody down.

( ) 10. A. recalls B. denies
C. concludes D. confesses

( ) 11. A. prospect B. responsibility
C. leadership D. protection

( ) 12. A. measure B. show
C. maintain D. ease

But as the groups got bigger and bigger, the amount of time spent in grooming activities also had to be ___13___ to maintain its effectiveness. Clearly, a more ___14___ kind of grooming was needed, and thus language evolved as a kind of vocal（有聲的）grooming which allowed humans to develop relationships with ever-larger groups by exchanging information over a wider network of individuals than would be possible by one-to-one __15__ contact.【2014 大陆上海卷】

( ) 13. A. saved B. extended
C. consumed D. gained

( ) 14. A. common B. efficient
C. scientific D. thoughtful

( ) 15. A. indirect B. daily
C. physical D. secret

Test 19 詳解

（2014 大陸上海卷）

Research has shown ***that*** *two-thirds of human conversation is taken up* [***not*** *with discussion of the cultural or political problems of the day,*

研究顯示，人類三分之二的對話不是討論當時文化或政治的問題，

two-thirds *n.* 三分之二

幾分之幾的寫法：數字（分子）– 序數（分母），分子是二以上，表示分母的序數要加 s，如：one-fifth（五分之一）、three-fourths（四分之三）。

take up 主要意思是「拿起；拾起」，在這裡作「佔用」解。

be taken up with 被…佔用　　***not*** A ***but*** B 不是 A 而是 B

of the day 當時的

not *heated debates about films we've just watched* or *books we've just finished reading*, ***but*** *plain and simple gossip.*]
1

不是關於我們剛看完的電影，或是剛讀完的書的激烈辯論，而是不折不扣的閒聊。
1

heated〔ˈhitɪd〕*adj.* 激烈的 debate〔dɪˈbet〕*n.* 辯論

plain 和 simple 是同義詞，都可以指「明白的；簡單的」，放在一起寫成 ***plain and simple*** 是副詞片語，表示「完完全全；不折不扣」(= *absolutely*)。

1. (**C**) 依句意，選 (C) ***gossip***〔ˈgɑsəp〕*n.* 閒聊。
   而 (A) claim〔klem〕*n.* 宣稱；要求，
   (B) description〔dɪˈskrɪpʃən〕*n.* 描述，
   (D) 語言，則不合句意。

Language is our greatest treasure *as a species*, ***and*** what do we *habitually* (2) do with it?

語言是我們身爲人類最重要的寶藏，而我們向來 (2) 會用它來做什麼呢？

注意：species（物種）雖然字尾有 s，但它是「單複數同形」。

2. (**B**) 依句意，選 (B) ***habitually***〔həˈbɪtʃuəlɪ〕*adv.* 習慣上。
   habit（習慣）+ ual (*adj.*) + ly (*adv.*)
   而 (A) occasionally〔əˈkeʒənḷɪ〕*adv.* 偶爾；有時候，
   (C) independently〔ˌɪndɪˈpɛndəntlɪ〕*adv.* 獨立地，
   (D) originally〔əˈrɪdʒənḷɪ〕*adv.* 最初；原本，則不合句意。

We gossip. About others' behaviour ***and*** private lives, [*such as who's doing what with whom, who's in and who's out*—***and*** *why*; *how to deal with difficult* social *situations involving children*, *lovers*, *and colleagues*.]
3

我們會閒聊。關於他人的行爲和私生活，像是誰跟誰做了什麼，誰時髦，誰過時——以及爲什麼；如何處理和小孩、情人，以及同事相關而困難的社交場面。
3

behaviour（行爲）是英式拼法，美式拼法是 behavior。

involve 常見的意思是「使牽涉在內」，如：Don't involve me in your quarrel.（別把我牽扯進你們的爭吵中。）這裡引申作「與…有關」解。

situations *involving* 是從 situations *which involve* 省略關代 *which* 而來的分詞片語。

in（ɪn）*adj.* 流行的；時髦的　　out（taʊt）*adj.* 過時的

deal with 應付；處理

colleague（ˈkɑlig）*n.* 同事（= *co-worker*）

3.（**A**）依句意，選 (A) ***social***（ˈsoʃəl）*adj.* 社會的；社交的。
而 (B) political（pəˈlɪtɪkḷ）*adj.* 政治的，
(C) historical（hɪsˈtɔrɪkḷ）*adj.* 歷史的，
(D) cultural（ˈkʌltʃərəl）*adj.* 文化的，則不合句意。

So why are we keen on gossiping? Are we *just* natural wasters, *of both time and words*?

所以我們爲何熱中閒聊？我們只是天生會浪費時間和話語的人嗎？

keen（熱中的）和介系詞 on 連用，表示「熱中於…」。
word 原本是「字；單字」，這裡是複數形，作「言語；話」解。
如：a man of few words（話少的人）。

4.（**D**）依句意，選 (D) ***waster***〔ˈwestɚ〕*n.* 浪費的人。
而 (A) admirer〔ədˈmaɪrɚ〕*n.* 仰慕者，
(B) master〔ˈmæstɚ〕*n.* 主人；大師，
(C) 使用者，則不合句意。

Or do we talk *a lot* about nothing *in particular* *simply to avoid facing up to the really important issues of life*?

或是我們漫無目的地講話，只是要避免正視生活中重要的問題嗎？

simply 是 simple（簡單的）的副詞，但是 simply 除了表示「簡單地」，還可作「只是；僅僅」（= *only*）解。
in particular 尤其；特別地（= *particularly* = *especially*）
face up to 勇敢地面對；正視 issue〔ˈɪʃjʊ〕*n.* 議題；問題

That's not the case *according to Professor Robin Dunbar. In fact, in his latest book, Grooming, Gossip and the Evolution of Language*, the psychologist says *gossip is one of these really vital issues.*
5

根據羅賓•鄧巴教授所說，眞相並非如此。事實上，在他最新的作品《哈著拉與抓虱》中，該心理學家說，閒聊是這些極爲重要的問題之一。
5

case 的主要意思是「案例；情形」，而 the case 則是作「眞相；實情」解。

Robin Dunbar〔'rɑbɪn dʌn'bɑr〕*n.* 羅賓•鄧巴

in fact 事實上　　latest〔'letɪst〕*adj.* 最新的

groom〔grum〕*v.* 使整潔；梳理毛髮

evolution〔,ɛvə'luʃən〕*n.* 進展；演化

Grooming, Gossip and the Evolution of Language 《刷毛、閒聊和語言的演化》【此中文翻譯書名爲《哈拉與抓虱》】

psychologist〔saɪ'kɑlədʒɪst〕*n.* 心理學家

5. (**A**) 依句意，選 (A) ***vital***〔'vaɪtl̩〕*adj.* 極爲重要的。
vit (*life*) + al (*adj.*)，跟生命相關，就是「非常重要的」(= *essential*)，名詞爲 vitality〔vaɪ'tælətɪ〕*n.* 活力。
而 (B) sensitive〔'sɛnsətɪv〕*adj.* 敏感的，
(C) ideal〔aɪ'diəl〕*adj.* 理想的，(D) 困難的，則不合句意。

Dunbar rejects the traditional view ***that*** *language was developed by men at an early stage of social development in order to organize their manly hunting activities more effectively*, ***or*** *even to promote the exchange of poetic stories about their origins and the supernatural.*
6

鄧巴反對這傳統的觀點：認爲語言是由男人在社會演變的早期所發展出來，爲了要更有效地組織男性的狩獵活動，或者甚至要是促進交流富有詩意，並關於男性起源和超自然現象的故事。
6

that 引導名詞子句，做 view（觀點；看法）的同位語。

or（或者）爲對等連接詞，連接 to organize 和 to promote。

traditional〔trəˈdɪʃənl̩〕*adj.* 傳統的　　stage〔stedʒ〕*n.* 階級

organize〔ˈɔrgən͵aɪz〕*n.* 組織

manly〔ˈmænlɪ〕*adj.* 適合男人的；有男子氣概的

effectively〔əˈfɛktɪvlɪ〕*adv.* 有效地

promote〔prəˈmot〕*v.* 促進

exchange〔ɪksˈtʃendʒ〕*n.* 交換；交流

poetic〔poˈɛtɪk〕*adj.* 詩的；有詩意的

origin〔ˈɔrədʒɪn〕*n.* 起源；開端

supernatural〔ˈsupɚ͵nætʃərəl〕*adj.* 超自然的

the supernatural 超自然現象

6. (**B**) re | ject 從字根分析，reject 的意思是「丟回去」，
back | throw 就是「拒絕；否認；反對」，依句意選 (B)。

而 (A) confirm〔kən'fɝm〕*v.* 證實，

(C) outline〔'aʊt,laɪn〕*v.* 畫…的輪廓；略述…的要點，

(D) broaden〔'brɔdn̩〕*v.* 拓展，則不合句意。

Instead he suggests ***that*** *language evolved among women.* We don't spend two-thirds of our time gossiping *just* ***because*** *we can talk*, argues Dunbar—*on the contrary*, he goes on to say, language evolved *specifically to allow us to gossip.*

7

他反而認爲語言是在女人之間演變而來。我們不會花三分之二的時間閒聊，只是因爲我們能夠講話，鄧巴主張——相反地，他繼續說，語言的發展是特意要讓我們閒聊。

7

instead〔ɪn'stɛd〕*adv.* 作爲代替；反而

suggest 的主要意思是「建議；暗示」，在此作「指出」解。

(= *indicate* = *show*)

evolve〔ɪ'vɑlv〕*v.* 發展；演變

specifically〔spɪ'sɪfɪklɪ〕*adv.* 特意地；特定地

7. (**C**) 依句意，選 (C) ***on the contrary*** 相反地 (= *contrarily*)。

而 (A) for instance「例如」，(B) in addition「此外」，

(D) as a result「因此」，則不合句意。

Dunbar arrived at his cheery theory *by studying the behaviour of higher primates, such as monkeys.*
8

藉由研究較高階靈長類動物，像是猴子的習性，鄧巴興高采烈地獲得他的理論。
8

arrive at 原本爲「到達」，這裡引申爲「獲得」(= *reach* = *come to*)。其他類似的說法有：arrive at a decision「做出決定」，arrive at a compromise「達成妥協」，arrive at a conclusion「下結論」等。

8.(**D**) 依句意，選(D) ***behaviour*** [bɪ'hevjɚ] *n.* 行爲；習性。

By means of grooming—cleaning the fur by brushing it, monkeys form groups [*with other individuals on **whom** they can rely for support in the event of some kind of conflict within the group **or** attack from outside it.*]
9

藉由梳理毛髮——用手清理毛髮，猴子和其他可以讓牠們依靠的猴子組成團體，萬一團體中發生某種衝突，或有外來的攻擊時，可以有援助。
9

means [minz] *n. pl.* 方法【單複數同形】

by means of 藉由(= *with the use of* = *through*)

fur〔 fɝ 〕*n.* 毛皮

individual〔ˌɪndəˈvɪdʒuəl 〕*n.* 個人；個體

on whom 的 on 是和 rely 連用的片語。

rely on 依靠（= *depend on* = *count on*）。

片語 in the event of 字面上是「在…的事件裡面」，引申爲「萬一發生」（= *in case of*）。

some〔 sʌm 〕*adj.* 某一　　conflict〔ˈkɑnflɪkt 〕*n.* 衝突

9.（**A**）依句意，選 (A) ***attack***〔 əˈtæk 〕*n.* 攻擊。
而 (B) contact〔ˈkɑntækt 〕*n.* 接觸；連結，
(C) inspection〔 ɪnˈspɛkʃən 〕*n.* 檢查，
(D) assistance〔 əˈsɪstəns 〕*n.* 協助，則不合句意。

As** we human beings evolve from a particular branch of the primate family*, Dunbar <u>concludes</u>[10] ***that *at one time in our history we did much the same.*

因爲我們人類是從靈長類動物科的特定支系演化而來，鄧巴<u>推斷</u>[10]我們在歷史上一度做幾乎一樣的事情。

as 可以表示「原因」，作「因爲」（= *since* = *seeing that*）解。

family（家庭），這裡是指「（生物學分類上的）科」，因爲人類是屬於靈長類動物「科」。而 branch 常見的意思是「樹枝」，這裡引申作「分支；（家族的）支系」解。

生物分類法：

kingdom *n.* 界	phylum〔ˈfaɪləm〕*n.* 門	
class *n.* 綱	order *n.* 目	family *n.* 科
genus〔ˈdʒinəs〕*n.* 屬	species *n.* 種	

at one time 一度（= *once* = *formerly*）

much the same 幾乎一樣

10.（**C**） con ¦ clude（together ¦ close） 從字根分析，conclude 的意思是「一起關上」，就是「下結論；推斷」，依句意，選 (C)。

而 (A) recall〔rɪˈkɔl〕*v.* 回想起，(B) deny〔dɪˈnaɪ〕*v.* 否認，(D) confess〔kənˈfɛs〕*v.* 承認，則不合句意。

Grouping *together* made sense [***because** the bigger the group, the greater the* protection (11) *it provided*; *on the other hand*, the bigger the group, the greater the stresses *of living close to others*.]

聚集在一起是很合理的，因爲團體越大，就能提供越大的保護(11)；另一方面來說，團體越大，鄰近他人生活的壓力就更大。

make sense 有道理；合情合理

「the + 比較級, …the + 比較級」表「越…就越～」

如：***The more*** he has, ***the more*** he wants.

（他擁有的越多，想要的就越多。）

on the other hand 另一方面來說（= *from another standpoint*）

stress〔strɛs〕*n.* 壓力　close〔klos〕*adv.* 接近地；靠近地

11. (**D**) 依句意，選 (D) ***protection*** (prəˈtɛkʃən) *n.* 保護。
而 (A) prospect (ˈprɑspɛkt) *n.* 希望，
(B) responsibility (ˌrɪspɑnsəˈbɪlətɪ) *n.* 責任，
(C) leadership (ˈlidɚˌʃɪp) *n.* 領導能力，則不合句意。

Grooming helped to ease (12) the pressure ***and*** calm everybody down.

梳理毛髮幫助減輕(12)壓力，使所有人鎮定。

pressure (ˈprɛʃɚ) *n.* 壓力　　***calm** sb. **down*** 使某人鎮定

12. (**D**) 依句意，選 (D) ***ease*** (iz) *v.* 減輕 (= *relieve* = *lessen*)。
而 (A) measure (ˈmɛʒɚ) *v.* 測量，(B) show (ʃo) *v.* 顯示，
(C) maintain (menˈten) *v.* 維持，則不合句意。

***But as** the groups got bigger and bigger*, the amount of time *spent in grooming activities also* had to be extended (13) *to maintain its effectiveness.*

但是隨著團體越來越大，花在梳理毛髮的時間必須要延長(13)，以維持它的效用。

as (隨著) 引導副詞子句，修飾動詞片語 ***have to be extented***。
effectiveness (əˈfɛktɪvnɪs) *n.* 效用

13. (**B**) ex | tend (out | stretch) 從字根分析，extend 的意思是「向外伸展」，也就是「延長」，依句意，選(B)。

而 (A) save「節省」，(C) consume〔kən'sum〕*v.* 消耗，(D) gain〔gen〕*v.* 獲得，則不合句意。

Clearly, a *more* efficient kind *of grooming* was needed, ***and*** *thus* language evolved as a kind *of vocal grooming*…

很明顯地，需要一個更有效率的梳理毛髮的方式，因此語言便演化成爲一種有聲梳理毛髮的方式，…
14

14. (**B**) ef | fic | ient (ex(out) | do | *adj.*) 從字根分析，efficient 的意思是「往外做」，做得多就是「有效率的」，依句意，選(B)。

而 (A) common〔'kɑmən〕*adj.* 常見的，
(C) scientific〔,saɪən'tɪfɪk〕*adj.* 科學的，
(D) thoughtful〔'θɔtfəl〕*adj.* 體貼的，則不合句意。

[***which*** *allowed humans to develop relationships with ever-larger groups by exchanging information over a wider network of individuals* ***than*** *would be possible by one-to-one* *physical contact.*]
15

這讓人類能和不斷變大的團體發展關係，藉由在更廣闊的人際網路上交流資訊，這不是透過一對一身體的接觸能達到的。
15

which 爲關係代名詞，引導形容詞子句，修飾先行詞 grooming（梳理毛髮）。
allow〔ə'laʊ〕*v.* 允許；使能夠
develop〔dɪ'vɛləp〕*v.* 發展（= *improve* = *expand* = *enlarge* = *extend* = *broaden*）
relationship〔rɪ'leʃən,ʃɪp〕*n.* 關係
ever 爲副詞，在此表示「不斷地」（= *constantly*）。
information〔,ɪnfɚ'meʃən〕*n.* 資訊
最後一句也可寫成：by exchanging information over a wider network of individuals than ***what*** would be possible by one-to-one physical contact.【準關代 than 後面接的 what 可省略，詳見「文法寶典」p.159】
over〔'ovɚ〕*prep.* 在…各處；遍及（= *in many parts of*）
network〔'nɛt,wɝk〕*n.* 網路
one-to-one *adj.* 一對一的（= *one-on-one*）

15.（**C**）依句意，選(C) ***physical***〔'fɪzɪkḷ〕*adj.* 身體的。
而 (A) indirect〔,ɪndə'rɛkt〕*adj.* 間接的，
(B) daily〔'delɪ〕*adj.* 日常的，
(D) secret〔'sikrɪt〕*adj.* 祕密的，則不合句意。

Test 20

Read the following passage and choose the best answer for each blank from the list below.

There is nothing that man fears more than the touch of the __1__. He wants to see what is reaching towards him, and to be able to recognize or at least classify it. Man always tends to avoid physical contact with anything strange. In the dark, the fear of an unexpected touch can mount to panic. Even clothes give __2__ security: it is easy to tear them and pierce through to the naked, smooth, defenseless flesh of the victim.

( ) 1. A. dead B. infamous
C. past D. unknown

( ) 2. A. ample B. extra
C. insufficient D. partial

All the distances which men create round themselves are __3__ by this fear. They shut themselves in houses which no one may enter, and only there feel some measure of security. The fear of burglars is not only the fear of being robbed, but also the fear of a sudden and unexpected clutch out of the darkness.

( ) 3. A. assaulted　　B. dictated
C. engaged　　D. implicated

The __4__ being touched remains with us when we go about among people; the way we move in a busy street, in restaurants, on trains or buses, is governed by it. Even when we are standing next to them and are able to watch and examine them closely, we avoid actual contact if we can. If we do not avoid it, it is because we feel we are __5__ someone, and then both of us can be comfortable.

( ) 4. A. delight of　　B. distaste for
C. feeling about　　D. release from

( ) 5. A. bored of　　B. familiar with
C. grateful to　　D. sorry for

We are dealing with a human tendency as deep-seated as it is alert and cunning. This tendency can be seen in the promptness with which an apology is offered for an unintentional contact, the tension with which it is awaited, our violent and sometimes even physical reaction when it is not forthcoming, the __6__ we feel for the offender, even when we cannot be certain who it is. Indeed, our human consciousness is inextricably bound by a whole knot of shifting and intensely reactions to an __7__ touch.【2015 日本早稻田大學】

( ) 6. A. antipathy B. disappointment
C. greed D. hesitation

( ) 7. A. alien B. earnest
C. innocent D. unfortunate

Test 20 詳解

(2015 日本早稻田大學)

There is nothing [***that*** *man fears more* ***than*** *the touch of the unknown.*] He wants to see ***what*** *is reaching towards him*, ***and*** to be able to recognize ***or*** *at least* classify it.
1

沒有比觸碰未知的東西更讓人害怕了。他想要看到什麼東西正在接近他，並能夠認出，或至少能分類它。
1

fear〔fɪr〕*v. n.* 害怕；恐懼　　touch〔tʌtʃ〕*n.* 觸碰
reach〔ritʃ〕*v.* 伸；達到
towards〔tordz〕*prep.* 朝向；接近　　***be able to V.*** 能夠～
recognize〔ˈrɛkəgˌnaɪz〕*v.* 認出
at least 至少　　classify〔ˈklæsəˌfaɪ〕*v.* 分類

1.(**D**) 依句意，選 (D) ***unknown***〔ʌnˈnon〕*adj.* 未知的；不明的。
the + *adj.* = 複數名詞【詳見「文法寶典」p.219】
the unknown 未知的事物（= *unknown things*）
而 (A) dead〔dɛd〕*adj.* 死亡的，
(B) infamous〔ˈɪnfəməs〕*adj.* 惡名昭彰的（= *notorious*），
(C) past〔pæst〕*adj.* 過去的，則不合句意。

Man *always* tends to avoid physical contact *with anything strange*. *In the dark*, the fear *of an unexpected touch* can mount to panic.

人總是傾向避免和任何奇怪的東西有肢體上的接觸。在黑暗中，意外碰觸的恐懼可能會加劇成恐慌。

tend to V. 傾向～；常常～　　avoid〔əˈvɔɪd〕*v.* 避免

physical〔ˈfɪzɪkl̩〕*adj.* 身體的　　contact〔ˈkɑntækt〕*n.* 接觸

in the dark 在黑暗中

unexpected〔ˌʌnɪkˈspɛktɪd〕*adj.* 意外的；突然的

mount〔maʊnt〕*v.* 上升；增強；加劇

panic〔ˈpænɪk〕*n.* 恐慌

Even clothes give insufficient security: it is easy to tear them **and** pierce through to the naked, smooth, defenseless flesh *of the victim.*

甚至是衣服都無法提供足夠的安全感；衣服很容易就可以撕破，並穿透到受害者赤裸、平滑、毫無保護的肌膚。

clothes〔kloz〕*n. pl.* 衣服

security〔sɪˈkjʊrətɪ〕*n.* 安全；安心

tear〔tɛr〕*v.* 撕裂　　pierce〔pɪrs〕*v.* 刺；穿透

naked〔ˈnekɪd〕*adj.* 裸露的；無遮蔽的

smooth〔smuð〕*adj.* 平滑的；光滑的

defenseless〔dɪˈfɛnslɪs〕*adj.* 無防備的；沒有保護的
flesh〔flɛʃ〕*n.* 肉體；肌膚　　victim〔ˈvɪktɪm〕*n.* 受害者

2. (**C**) 依句意，選 (C) ***insufficient***〔ˌɪnsəˈfɪʃənt〕*adj.* 不足的。
in (*not*) + sufficient (足夠的) = insufficient
(= *inadequate*〔ɪnˈædəkwɪt〕)。
而 (A) ample〔ˈæmpḷ〕*adj.* 充足的 (= *enough*)，
(B) extra〔ˈɛkstrə〕*adj.* 額外的，
(D) partial〔ˈpɑrʃəl〕*adj.* 部分的；偏袒的，則不合句意。

All the distances ***which*** *men create round themselves* are *dictated* *by this fear.*
3

人在他們周圍創造的所有距離，都是由這樣的恐懼所支配。
3

distance〔ˈdɪstəns〕*n.* 距離　　create〔krɪˈet〕*v.* 創造
round〔raʊnd〕*prep.* 環繞 (= *around*)

3. (**B**) 依句意，選 (B) ***dictate***〔ˈdɪktet〕*v.* 決定；支配。
dict (*say*) + ate (*v.*) = dictate，能說話就是「決定；支配」。
而 (A) assault〔əˈsɔlt〕*v.* 攻擊；突襲 (= *attack*)，
(C) engage〔ɪnˈgedʒ〕*v.* 從事；參與 < *in* >，
(D) implicate〔ˈɪmplɪˌket〕*v.* 牽涉 (= *involve*)，
則不合句意。

They shut themselves in houses ***which*** *no one may enter*, ***and only there*** feel some measure *of security*. The fear *of burglars* is ***not only*** the fear *of being robbed*, ***but also*** the fear *of a sudden* ***and*** *unexpected clutch out of the darkness*.

他們把自己關在房子裡，沒人可以進入，並只有在那裡才感受到些許的安全感。對竊賊的恐懼不只是害怕被搶劫，還有害怕在黑暗中，突然無法預期地被緊抓著。

shut〔ʃʌt〕*v.* 關閉　　***shut** sb. **in**…* 把某人關在…
some〔sʌm〕*adj.* 某個　　measure〔ˈmɛʒɚ〕*n.* 數量；程度
burglar〔ˈbɝglɚ〕*n.* 竊賊
not only…but also～ 不只…而且～
rob〔rɑb〕*v.* 搶奪；搶劫
sudden〔ˈsʌdn̩〕*adj.* 突然的；出乎意料的
clutch〔klʌtʃ〕*n.* 緊抓　　***out of*** 來自
darkness〔ˈdɑrknɪs〕*n.* 黑暗

The distaste *for being touched* remains with us *when we go about among people*; the way [*we move in a busy street*, *in restaurants*, *on trains or buses*,] is governed *by it*.
4

當我們在人群中走動時，討厭被碰觸的感受伴隨著我們；我們在熱鬧的街道上、餐廳裡、火車上，或是公車上行動的方式，都是受到這厭惡感所主宰。

remain〔rɪ'men〕*v.* 保持；繼續　***remain with*** 伴隨
go about 到處走動　move〔muv〕*v.* 移動；行動
busy〔'bɪzɪ〕*adj.* 忙碌的；熱鬧的
govern〔'gʌvən〕*v.* 決定；支配；主宰

4.（**B**）依句意，選 (B) ***distaste for***「對…的厭惡」。
distaste〔dɪs'test〕*n.* 不喜歡；討厭；厭惡
而 (A) delight of「…的喜悅」，delight〔dɪ'laɪt〕*n.* 喜悅，
(C) feeling about「…的感受」，
(D) release from「從…釋放」，release〔rɪ'lis〕*n.* 釋放；解除，則不合句意。

[*Even **when** we are standing next to them **and** are able to watch **and** examine them closely*,] we avoid actual contact ***if** we can*. ***If** we do not avoid it*, it is ***because** we feel we are familiar with* (5) *someone*, ***and** then* both *of us* can be comfortable.

甚至當我們站在他們旁邊，並能夠注視和仔細觀察他們，我們會避免實際上的接觸，如果可能的話。如果我們無法避免，這是因爲我們熟悉某人，而且我們兩人都感到很自在。

next to 在…的旁邊　　watch〔wɑtʃ〕*v.* 注視
examine〔ɪɡ'zæmɪn〕*v.* 仔細觀察（= *observe*）
closely〔'kloslɪ〕*adv.* 專心地
actual〔'æktʃuəl〕*adj.* 實際的
comfortable〔'kʌmfətəbḷ〕*adj.* 舒服的；自在的

5.（**B**）依句意，選(B) ***familiar with***「和…熟悉」。
familiar〔fə'mɪljə〕*adj.* 熟悉的
而 (A) bored of「對…厭倦」，
(C) grateful to「感激（某人）」，
grateful〔'gretfəl〕*adj.* 感激的（= *thankful*），
(D) sorry for「對…感到遺憾」，則不合句意。

We are dealing with a human tendency as deep-seated ***as** it is*

*alert **and** cunning*. This tendency can be seen *in the*

*promptness with **which** an apology is offered for an*

unintentional contact, *the tension with **which** it is awaited*, *our*

*violent **and** sometimes even physical reaction **when** it is not*

forthcoming, *the antipathy we feel for the offender, even **when***

*we cannot be certain **who** it is.*

6

我們正在討論的是一項人類的習性，既根深蒂固也警覺又靈巧。這樣的習性可以顯現在無心碰觸他人時，迅速表示道歉的時候，焦急等待道歉的時候，當沒有得到道歉時，我們表現出激烈的，有時候甚至是肢體上的反應的時候，我們對冒犯者感到反感的時候，甚至當我們無法確認誰是冒犯者的時候。
(6: 反感)

deal with 處理；討論　tendency (ˈtɛndənsɪ) *n.* 傾向；習性
deep-seated (ˈdipˈsitɪd) *adj.* 根深蒂固的 (= *deep-rooted*)
as…as (S + be) ~ 既…也~　alert (əˈlɝt) *adj.* 警覺的
cunning (ˈkʌnɪŋ) *adj.* 狡猾的；靈巧的
promptness (ˈprɑmptnəs) *n.* 迅速；敏捷
with promptness 迅速地 (= *promptly*)
apology (əˈpɑlədʒɪ) *n.* 道歉　offer (ˈɔfɚ) *v.* 提供；表示
unintentional (ˌʌnɪnˈtɛnʃənl̩) *adj.* 不是故意的；無心的
tension (ˈtɛnʃən) *n.* 緊張；焦急
with tension 緊張地；焦急地　await (əˈwet) *v.* 等待
violent (ˈvaɪələnt) *adj.* 激烈的
reaction (rɪˈækʃən) *n.* 反應
forthcoming (ˈforθˈkʌmɪŋ) *adj.* 即將到來的；可得到的
offender (əˈfɛndɚ) *n.* 冒犯者　certain (ˈsɝtn̩) *adj.* 確定的

6. (**A**) 依句意，選 (A) ***antipathy*** (ænˈtɪpəθɪ) *n.* 反感；討厭。
anti (*against*) + pathy (*feeling*)，反抗的感覺，就是「反感」(= *dislike*)。
而 (B) disappointment (ˌdɪsəˈpɔɪntmənt) *n.* 失望，
(C) greed (grid) *n.* 貪心，
(D) hesitation (ˌhɛzəˈteʃən) *n.* 猶豫，則不合句意。

Indeed, our human consciousness is *inextricably* bound *by a whole knot of shifting and intensely sensitive reactions to an <u>innocent</u> touch.*
7

的確，我們人類的知覺是和另一完整的反應環節緊密結合的，這些反應是不穩定的，並對一個<u>無惡意的</u>碰觸也是非常敏感的。
7

indeed〔 ɪn'did 〕*adv.* 的確
consciousness〔'kɑnʃəsnɪs 〕*n.* 意識；知覺
inextricably〔ˌɪnɪk'strɪkəblɪ 〕*adv.* 解不開地；緊密地
bound〔 baʊnd 〕*v.* 綑綁；使關係密切【bind 的過去分詞】
whole〔 hol 〕*adj.* 整個的；完整的
knot〔 nɑt 〕*n.* 結；結合；節
shifting〔'ʃɪftɪŋ 〕*adj.* 變動的；不穩定的（= *unstable* ）
intensely〔 ɪn'tɛnslɪ 〕*adv.* 強烈地；非常
sensitive〔'sɛnsətɪv 〕*adj.* 敏感的

7.（ **C** ）依句意，選 (C) ***innocent***〔'ɪnəsn̩t 〕*adj.* 天真的；沒有惡意的（= *unintentional* = *inoffensive* ）。
而 (A) alien〔'eljən 〕*adj.* 外國的；陌生的，
(B) earnest〔'ɝnɪst 〕*adj.* 認眞的，
(D) unfortunate〔 ʌn'fɔrtʃənɪt 〕*adj.* 不幸的，則不合句意。

D 16. A. permits 許可証 B. interest
C. talent 天分 D. clothes

He tried out for the football team, but the coach turned him down for being too small.

B 17. A. on B. for
C. in D. with

A 18. A. small B. flexible 有彈性的
C. optimistic 樂觀的 D. outgoing 外向的

try out for 參加～的甄選
couch n. 教練 v. 指導
turn down 拒絕

During this period Dale was slowly developing an inferiority 自卑 complex 感情結, which his mother knew 插入語 could prevent him from achieving his real potential.

prevent / stop / keep / prohibit / discourage / deter / hinder / restrain … from 阻止

achieve one's potential 發揮潛力
= realize one's potential

C 19. A. gaining B. achieving
C. developing D. obtaining

A 20. A. prevent B. protect
C. save D. free

develop v. 發展；顯現
gain confidence 增加自信心

She suggested that Dale join the debate 辯論 team 隊, believing that practice 練習 in speaking 演說 could give him the confidence and recognition that he needed.

Dale took his mother's advice, tried desperately, and after several attempts finally made it.

A 21. A. suggested B. demanded 要求
C. required 要求 D. insisted 堅持

B 22. A. presence 存在；出席 B. practice
C. patience 耐心 D. potential 潛力

C 23. A. hopefully 有希望地 B. certainly 必定
C. finally D. naturally 自然地

※ Take my advice, and you can make it. (聽我的勸,你就會成功)

Trust me, you can make it. (相信我,你會成功。)

This proved to be a turning point in his life.

D 24. A. key B. breaking
C. basic D. turning

這証明了是他生命中的轉捩點。

turning point 轉捩點

Speaking before groups (團體) did help him gain the confidence he needed.

D 25. A. progress (進步) B. experience
C. competence (能力) D. confidence (自信;信心)

By the time Dale was a senior, he had won every top honor in speech.

C 26. A. horse-riding (騎馬) B. football
C. speech 演講 D. farming (農耕)

top honor 最高榮譽
= top prize

Now other students were coming to him for coaching and they, in turn, were winning contests.

C 27. A. in return (作為回報) B. in brief (簡言之)
C. in turn (依序地;後來) D. in fact

in turn 依序地;後來;轉動

Out of this early struggle to overcome (克服) his feelings of inferiority, Dale came to understand that the ability to express an idea to an audience builds a person's confidence.

B 28. A. convey (傳達) B. overcome (克服)
C. understand D. build

A 29. A. express B. stress 強調
C. contribute (貢獻) D. repeat (重複)

out of 從~中 (= from)

express v. 表達 (= convey)

And, with it, Dale knew he could do anything he wanted to do —— and so could others.

D 30. A. besides B. beyond C. life D. with

with 表「具有」(= having)

破折號(——)表總括全句

[詳見文家 P. 42]

What do we do with our hands? (手有什麼用?)

What do we do with English? (英文有什麼用?)

Test 4

Joe Simpson and Simon Yates [jets]

喬．辛普森　賽門．葉茨

were the first people to climb....

... the west face of the Siula Grande

西面　修拉山 大

in the Andes ['ændiz] mountains. [sɪ'ulə grænde]

安地斯山脈

They reached the top successfully,

but on their way back conditions were very difficult.

C 31. A. hurriedly B. carefully C. successfully D. early

A 32. A. difficult B. similar C. special D. normal

Joe fell and broke his leg.

They both knew that if Simon continued alone, he would probably get back safely.

D 33. A. climbed B. worked C. rested D. continued

B 34. A. unwillingly B. safely C. slowly D. regretfully

But Simon decided to risk his life and try to lower Joe down the mountain on a rope.

D 35. A. fortune B. time C. health D. life

risk one's life 冒著某人的生命危險

As they went down (下山), the weather got worse.

36. A. lay B. settled
C C. went D. looked

Then more trouble occurred.
然後

37. A. damage B. storm
D C. change D. trouble

They couldn't see or hear each other and, by mistake, Simon lowered his friend over the edge of a precipice.

precipice [ˈpresəpɪs] n. 峭壁
[諧音：不拉繩必死]
他們把他的朋友從峭壁邊緣垂下去

38. A. by mistake
A B. by chance 偶然地
C. by choice 出於自願
D. by luck 碰運氣

by mistake 失誤；意外地
= by accident
= accidentally

It was impossible [for Joe to climb back or for Simon to pull him up.]

39. A. unnecessary
D B. practical
C. important
D. impossible

Joe's weight was pulling Simon slowly toward the precipice.

40. A. height B. weight
B C. strength D. equipment

Finally, [after more than an hour in the dark and the icy cold,] Simon had to make a decision.

41. A. Finally B. Patiently
A 最後(= Eventually)
C. Surely D. Quickly

42. A. stand back 後退
C B. take a test
C. make a decision
D. hold on 堅持下去

in the dark 在黑暗中
in the cold 在寒冷中
in the hot (×)
in the heat 在炎熱的天氣中

In tears, he cut the rope.
淚流滿面

Joe fell into a huge crevasse in the ice below.
[krəˈvæs] n. 裂縫 [過肥死，過肥的人掉進裂縫會死]

43. A. jumped B. fell
B C. escaped D. backed